"Are You Sure You Want To Make Love With Me?"

"Yes," Sabrina said with no hesitation.

Reese's body screamed, *Take this woman, now!* But his mind cautioned him to warn her. She was the kind of woman who deserved a devoted guy and a wedding. He wasn't that man.

"It can only be for tonight."

"I know. I want to be with you," she said.

Then Sabrina moved forward and touched his cheek. No one had ever touched him with such tenderness, such exquisite sweetness. And Reese knew instantly that he'd never be satisfied with just one night....

Dear Reader,

This April of our 20th anniversary year, Silhouette will continue to shower you with powerful, passionate, provocative love stories!

Cait London offers an irresistible MAN OF THE MONTH, *Last Dance,* which also launches her brand-new miniseries FREEDOM VALLEY. Sparks fly when a strong woman tries to fight her feelings for the rugged man who's returned from her past. *Night Music* is another winner from BJ James's popular BLACK WATCH series. Read this touching story about two wounded souls who find redeeming love in each other's arms.

Anne Marie Winston returns to Desire with her emotionally provocative *Seduction, Cowboy Style,* about an alpha male cowboy who seeks revenge by seducing his enemy's sister. In *The Barons of Texas: Jill* by Fayrene Preston, THE BARONS OF TEXAS miniseries offers another feisty sister, and the sexy Texan who claims her.

Desire's theme promotion THE BABY BANK, in which interesting events occur on the way to the sperm bank, continues with Katherine Garbera's *Her Baby's Father.* And Barbara McCauley's scandalously sexy miniseries SECRETS! offers another tantalizing tale with *Callan's Proposition,* featuring a boss who masquerades as his secretary's fiancé.

Please join in the celebration of Silhouette's 20th anniversary by indulging in all six Desire titles—which will fulfill *your* every desire!

Enjoy!

Joan Marlow Golan

Joan Marlow Golan
Senior Editor, Silhouette Desire

Please address questions and book requests to:
Silhouette Reader Service
U.S.: 3010 Walden Ave., P.O. Box 1325, Buffalo, NY 14269
Canadian: P.O. Box 609, Fort Erie, Ont. L2A 5X3

Her Baby's Father
KATHERINE GARBERA

Silhouette Desire

Published by Silhouette Books

America's Publisher of Contemporary Romance

SILHOUETTE BOOKS

ISBN 0-373-76289-5

HER BABY'S FATHER

Copyright © 2000 by Katherine Garbera

This edition published by arrangement with Harlequin Books S.A.

Visit Silhouette at www.eHarlequin.com

Printed in U.S.A.

KATHERINE GARBERA

Writing romance novels is a dream come true for Katherine Garbera. As a child she was never without a book and once gave up pleasure reading for Lent—"It was the longest forty days of my life." She wrote her first novel to prove to herself that she could do it, and was hooked on writing. She is a past winner of the Georgia Romance Writers Maggie Award and a member of Romance Writers of America. When she is not writing, Katherine spends time with her husband of ten years and their two children. She also enjoys counted cross-stitch, playing the flute, swimming and tae kwon do, which she does with her seven-year-old daughter. She loves to hear from her readers, and you can write to her at P.O. Box 1806, Davenport, FL 33836.

This book is dedicated to the memory of
Rose Wilkinson, my grandmother. Thanks for sharing
your love of the past and of our heritage with me.
Thanks for making me feel like the most beautiful girl
in the world, even though I'm not, and mostly thank you
for your love. I miss you!

❖❖❖❖❖❖

Acknowledgments

Thanks to Bob Allen for sharing his knowledge of boats
with me and taking time out of his busy schedule to
answer all of my questions. Any errors in nautical terms
are my own.

Because this story is at its heart about family, I want to
thank mine for all the gifts they've given me. My
parents, who've given me the gift of time to write by
watching my children. My sisters for giving me the gifts
of love and support and reminding me why we need our
family around us always. My grandfather, who is my
connection with the past and a great lover of all sports.
My paternal grandmother, who has given me a friend
to share reading with. Lastly, my husband, who reminds
me every day why the love of a good man is important
to all of us.

One
_____

She was late. Reese Howard was punctual to a fault. He'd grown up always missing appointments and being left behind, so it was a passion of his. In fact, it was a pet peeve and it added fuel to the simmering fire he felt toward this assignment.

All his life he'd worked to break out of the mold his childhood had shaped for him. Though he hadn't been destined for success, success had become his. But at what price?

Not even thirty-five, and he had chronic high blood pressure; his doctor had recommended retirement due to a history of heart disease in his family and his workaholic habits. Instead of retiring, he'd changed career paths midstream, leaving a primo job at the *Los Angeles Times* as an investigative reporter. Going from a man in the thick of things to a fluff-article writer.

This new assignment for the Life-styles section of *California Magazine,* a lame story series titled ''Artificial Insemination—Wave of the Future,'' made him wince.

He glanced again at his watch, cursing this ridiculous assignment. He knew his anger was directed more toward himself and the circumstances that had led him here than at the late Ms. MacFadden.

It was a hot summer day. He wanted to be out on the *Time Lapse,* his thirty-foot yacht, skimming San Francisco Bay instead of lurking outside an artificial insemination clinic. The breeze blew across the bay, stirring the hair at the back of his neck. Reese leaned his head against the sun-warmed stone wall. Feeling older than he had a right to, he breathed deeply and tried to relax.

But he couldn't relax. He felt like a pervert—afraid someone would see him and think he was a donor.

It grated on him in a core way that sperm banks existed for single women. He understood how a couple experiencing infertility might need to visit a place like this, but a woman on her own—never. A man's duty was to get his mate pregnant.

Even as the thought rolled through his mind, he knew it was chauvinistic. But there was a reason why God had created two sexes and put them on Earth together, and it wasn't so that they could procreate without ever touching.

Though he wasn't domesticated and would probably never have any offspring, his male pride chafed at the idea of a woman having a child on her own. He knew a lot of men dropped the ball on the fatherhood front, but that didn't mean there weren't a lot of stand-up guys ready to sign on for the long haul. There were enough guys that sperm banks weren't necessary.

His magazine had arranged to pay for the procedure for a woman, Sabrina MacFadden, to ensure that she'd tell them all the details of her decision. She must be desperate—probably thirty-eight, never been with a man and looked as appealing as a tight end after a particularly grueling play-off game.

He'd left L.A. for this?

Squinting against the late-afternoon sun, he propped himself against the side of the building to wait for the MacFadden woman. A loud thumping beat of music drew his attention to the parking lot. A classic '69 Mustang convertible pulled neatly into a front parking spot.

The top was down and the driver wore a bright red scarf tied around her hair and big, flashy sunglasses. She stepped out of the car and removed the covering from her head. Long reddish-brown hair fell in waves around her shoulders. He wanted to bury his hands in her thick curls.

Oh, yeah.

She reached into the car, then pulled out a navy suit jacket. As she tugged it on, the silk shell she wore pulled tight across her breasts. Reese knew he should look away, but he couldn't.

The woman walked like a dream. Reese briefly

considered ditching the assignment and seducing her into going home with him. She was the embodiment of a dream he'd had when he'd been sixteen. His favorite classic car and a sexy woman, both in overdrive.

Pig, he thought.

The woman moving toward him had endless legs. They seemed to start at her armpits and go on forever. The straight skirt ended at mid-thigh and crept upward the tiniest bit with each step she took. He'd never seen such perfect thighs. He felt that she was a dream come to life. He fantasized about those legs as she strode toward him with the fluid grace of a dancer. Maybe this wasn't going to be a bad day, after all.

The fitted skirt molded to her hips like a second skin. Longing to caress her, he shoved his hands into his pockets. A shadow blocked her face from view, leaving the mundane detail of her identity to his fantasy.

He imagined they were on a deserted beach and she wore a skimpy bikini. Realistically, he assumed her body wouldn't be as good-looking under her clothes as it was dressed in that sexy bit of nothing his imagination had supplied, but his lusty mind filled in all the details. She would look like a cross between Cindy Crawford and Kathy Ireland, but not too perfect, because perfection was its own evil. She'd have the mind of a nuclear physicist and she'd bake like Betty Crocker, because every woman should know how to cook.

Knowing his eyes were masked by the mirrored

shades of his aviator sunglasses, he continued to ogle her body as she stopped in front of him. A soft summer breeze ruffled her hair and carried the scent of flowers to him.

"Excuse me?" she said.

Her designer sunglasses hid her eyes and half of her face, but her nose was perky. He liked that. With *her* body, classic features would have been overkill.

"Yes?"

"Are you Reese Howard?" she asked, the words reaching his ears in slow motion.

Ah, the fantasy continues. Maybe he'd been in the sun too long. Her mouth intrigued him. He had to shake off his lethargy. But more than anything he wanted to kiss those lips, especially her full bottom lip, which looked as if it were begging for a man's caress. To nibble there before delving deeper and exploring the secret recesses of her mouth. He wanted to feel that mouth move under his as he thoroughly plundered it.

"Yes, ma'am."

"*Great.* I'm Sabrina MacFadden. Sorry I'm late."

She held out her hand and he responded automatically with a handshake. The touch of her delicate fingers shot sparks from his arm to his groin. The sun must have made him dizzy, because never before had touching a woman had such an immediate reaction on his body. Her fingers were long and fine-boned. Her fragile, feminine grip made him feel like a big brute—a masculine warrior. It brought to the fore all of his gut instincts—conquer her and make her completely his.

She removed her sunglasses with her free hand. He stared into eyes the color of the deep Caribbean Sea where he'd spent last summer. Vulnerable eyes that seemed to invite him closer to her while begging him to stay away. Eyes that reminded him of home—not the house he'd spent his childhood in, but that deep sated feeling for which he'd always secretly longed.

Realizing he'd never responded to her, he muttered, "No problem. Let's go across the street to the Bay Side Café and we'll start our interview."

Big problem. This woman was messing with his libido and his protective instincts. He didn't like it. She was supposed to be older, more maidenly and about as tempting as three-day-old bread. She was young, sexy, vibrant; alive in a way he'd forgotten how to be.

The only time he came close to that feeling anymore was when he was doing something dangerous. Rappelling without a partner in the dead of night, driving his motorcycle through Devil's Pass at ninety, hanging on by sheer guts. A sense of purity around this woman reminded him of the fleetingness of his own life.

He cupped her elbow to help her across the street. She stiffened. Okay, he knew she didn't need help but he'd wanted to touch her. Longed to feel her smooth, elegant arm under his hand. He wanted to wrap his arm around her shoulders and pull her flush against his body.

Reese dropped her arm. Hell, he was a professional. He didn't get involved with his interview subjects. When the light changed and they crossed the street, he shortened his stride to allow her to walk comfortably. Mario, the owner, spotted him and gave him the thumbs-up sign when he saw Ms. MacFadden. Reese held her chair as she seated herself at the outdoor café.

She was the kind of woman men noticed, Reese realized. Certainly not the kind of woman who'd *have* to have a child on her own. If only she wanted to stay single and childless, he thought. He assured himself that once they sat down and talked she'd lose her appeal.

He'd played the field for a long time. He'd worked hard in L.A. but had partied hard as well. There had never been time for a serious relationship, which was fine with him. He acknowledged that most women seemed the same to him. There was no longer the thrill of meeting and discovering something new.

But here it was. And stronger than he'd ever experienced before because it was so unexpected. Like the excitement he'd found only in his former work, and in the danger he'd chased on sheer rock mountain faces and rivers of roiling white water. He hadn't felt this alive in a long, long time.

And a *woman* was making him feel that way.

Not a drugged-out street thug who mistook him for a cop, or even the wild ocean in the middle of an unexpected storm or dangerous rapids on the raging Colorado. It was a woman!

Please, God, let her be ditzy.

* * *

Sabrina MacFadden fiddled nervously with her water glass. Reese Howard was not the type of man she'd pictured. She hadn't expected to feel a spark of desire when they'd touched. She shook hands all the time in her role as secretary to the vice president of sales. It was the kind of job that demanded lots of interaction and hand-to-hand contact, but nothing, *nothing* had prepared her for the shock she'd felt. More like a sense of rightness. A feeling that she'd met the yin to her yang.

He should have been some stereotypical newspaperman who looked like he belonged in another era instead of the muscle-bound guy sitting across from her. This guy probably had never encountered an obstacle he couldn't conquer.

His biceps bulged when he pulled over an extra chair. She felt like a ninety-pound weakling despite the fact that she worked out. Well okay, jazzercise really only worked if you went every week, but still.

She'd never felt so feminine. Never been this close to a man whose testosterone level was so high she could almost smell it. He was a man's man. The kind of guy who could walk into a roughhouse-roadside bar and feel at home.

His touch at her elbow when they'd crossed the street had burned through her thin summer suit jacket. For a minute she'd forgotten why she'd given up on men. But the answer rushed back. There was no mythical Mr. Right waiting out there for her. Just good-looking guys ready for a "good time" and then goodbye. Reese Howard would be no different, she reminded herself firmly.

"Do you like latte?"

"Yes," she said. She'd become addicted to caffeine early in life when her maternal grandparents had fixed her "sweet coffee" in a demitasse.

He ordered fancy coffee for both of them, in a way that annoyed her. But she let it go because surely she'd annoyed him by being late. He probably needed to reestablish his position of control. Having worked with men throughout her career, she was used to the way they tried to hoard power and had learned to fight the big battles and let go of the little ones.

He propped his elbow on the table and watched her. It unnerved her. She wished she could see his eyes. Was he really looking at her? The mirrored shades showed her nothing but herself.

The woman looking back at her wasn't one she embraced. It was a breezy day. Her hair seemed to have a will of its own, which dictated that it writhe around her head like Medusa's snakes. Concerned that he'd give her a bad report to his boss, she tried unobtrusively to tame her hair with her hands.

Worry never solved anything. Calm down.

But she couldn't. So much rode on the outcome of their initial meeting. What if he went back to his editors and told them to find a different woman for the artificial insemination article? She'd have to find a way to pay for it herself, and money was tight right now because she was saving to buy a house on Mount Tam. And banks liked to see money in your account before they lent you more money.

The only thing she owned of real value was the

classic car her father had purchased for her the year she'd been born. And after his death two years ago she'd promised herself to never sell it. She would in an extreme emergency, but right now there was another option. An option that would bring her lifelong dream of being a mother to fruition.

She glanced out over the bay and remembered why she'd started making sacrifices. She had always wanted a large family, but her parents had been in their late forties when she'd been born and they hadn't been able to have any more children. She missed her mom and dad, craving the bond of family the way some people craved money and others coveted power.

She craved children because a large hole in the center of her soul couldn't be filled by work or dating. She needed to nurture a small being, to pass on the stories and skills she'd learned from her parents and leave behind a small piece of herself. And she wanted to start on her family before she was too old to enjoy a child.

Her failed marriage had proved the only way she'd have a family was to go out and create one herself. She needed the stability. She missed the love and caring. She wanted to be able to accomplish something meaningful before she died. She'd had one of her closest friends die last year from cancer. Sabrina felt everything happened for a reason. Marcia's death had convinced Sabrina it was time to make changes. *She wasn't going to live forever.*

The sun beat down on the back of her head, and despite an occasional breeze, she was hot. The sea

16

air smelled sweet and she wished she were on the beach. Maybe holding hands with her faceless dream man. The one who always showed up in her fantasies but never in real life.

She wanted every detail of this interview to be perfect. Hopefully, the reporter would be so impressed by her, that he would make his editor understand why it was so important she have a child. She must make up for the ground she'd lost by being late. The magazine hadn't paid for anything yet—this interview would be the deciding factor.

Once their lattes arrived, Reese removed a narrow pad from his back pocket. "Tell me about your decision to have a child by yourself."

He removed his sunglasses, and she found herself staring into eyes the color of the darkest night. They had to be brown, she thought, but they were so dark they seemed black. The lines of his face showed signs of hard living and time in the sun. She'd always been attracted to outdoorsy men. Reese Howard was rugged and drop-dead gorgeous—and he'd been eyeing her when she'd walked up to him.

"I'm lonely," she said at last, thinking of this past solitary Christmas. All of her friends spent the time with family, and though Kayla had insisted she'd be welcome with her family, Sabrina simply couldn't spend the holiday with her friend.

It would have demonstrated to Kayla and the world what Sabrina didn't have. It was then that she'd made her decision to have a child. The idea had been in her mind for months, but sitting in front

of the gaily decorated Christmas tree by herself had
focused her resolution.

He didn't write that down. He set a ratty-looking
pen on the table and leaned forward, bracing his
weight on his folded arms. The breeze kicked up
again and ruffled the hair that brushed the back of
his collar. He needed a haircut, she thought.

"Lonely how?" he asked, his voice raspy. The
kind of voice her faceless dream lover had. The sexy
tone made her shiver inside her coat and she rubbed
her arms to dispel the sensation.

She began to feel more at ease and practically
forgot that this wasn't a casual meeting between
friends, but a business interview. He made her feel
as if she were the only woman in the world. What
she had to say was important to him, she realized.
"I have no family. Everyone at work has a family,
some are close-knit, some complain about family
members, and I have no one."

He narrowed his eyes and looked out over the
bay. Sailboats, wind surfers and water skiers pep-
pered the water. "Are you an orphan?"

"Not really. But my parents died a few years
ago." She let the memory of her dad play through
her mind. He'd often smelled sweetly of pipe to-
bacco, and his embrace had always engulfed her,
making her feel cherished and safe in a way she
hadn't in a long time. And she missed her mom's
smile and warm understanding. She wanted one last
hug from them, but knew, of course, she could never
have it.

She longed to be a little person's security blanket.

The one thing that made a child feel safe in the middle of the night when scary monsters came to call. And later in life, when the teenage social scene left heartbreak, she wanted to soothe the hurt. She wanted to feel as if she was making a difference in someone's life the way her parents had in hers. But more important, she wanted to share the joy of living with someone else. *With family.*

"I'm sorry," he said. And she saw in his eyes that he really was. For an instant their gazes met and she felt that same current charge through her. Something shocking and unexpected, like a stream of warm water in the cool Pacific Ocean.

"Thanks. I still miss them," she said. Tears burned the backs of her eyes but didn't fall. She blinked several times and looked away.

"My dad is gone, too," he said.

"What about your mom?" she asked, though it wasn't her interview.

"She died giving birth to me," he said in a way that didn't encourage further questions.

She glanced back at him and was compelled to touch him. Taking his hand in hers, she rubbed her thumb over his knuckles. He stared at her for a long minute before finally turning away.

Sabrina looked down at their hands, startled again by his size. His hands were tanned where hers were pale. His skin calloused where hers was smooth. His touch comforting where her life had been lacking for so long.

She pulled her hand from his slowly, reluctant to stop touching him. Shoving her hands in her lap, she forced herself to be more businesslike. No matter how comfortable she felt with him, he wasn't her friend. He wasn't her soul mate no matter how much his deep eyes made him seem so. He wasn't anything more to her than a stranger.

"Why is having a child on your own terms so important to you?" he asked.

Sabrina looked out at the sea and gathered her thoughts. She knew why she wanted a baby, but she'd never put it into words. It was more a feeling of something that was missing.

"I'm not sure I'll say this right, but it's like there's this big part of me missing. My arms ache to hold a baby—not my friends' or co-workers', but my own."

She glanced up to see if he understood what she was trying to say. It was impossible to tell from his expression. Her feelings about the baby were tied closely to the woman she'd dreamed of being when she was eighteen and about to be married.

She remembered standing in a church filled with family and friends and staring down the aisle at the man she thought would love her forever. The man she thought would father all four of the children she dreamed of having.

Now she once again felt like a woman on the cusp of change. But this time she was in control—and finally on the edge of having her dream come true. All she had to do was convince the man sitting across from her to grant this wish.

She reached for her latte, then took a deep swallow. She felt as if she'd regained the ground she'd lost by her tardiness.

"One last question and we'll wrap this up," he said, giving her a grin that didn't reach his eyes.

"Why don't you want a man in your life?"

Two

Reese watched Sabrina choke on her coffee. Of course, he shouldn't have asked the question at all. He felt like a killer whale bearing down on a sea lion. It was the type of probing question his editor Jeff had warned him to be careful of asking when interviewing her.

Her aqua-blue eyes reflected her hurt and she blinked several times. He acknowledged that he wouldn't have asked in such a blunt way if she had been thirty-something, matronly and unappealing. While they'd sat in the sun-warmed sidewalk café, the bond between them had seemed to strengthen. As if their lives had been leading up to this moment and this meeting.

Electric shocks jumped between them each time

they touched. And Reese felt off balance, as if a quake rolled through him, waking him from a slumber he hadn't realized he'd been in. A slumber that had allowed him safety in relationships and safety in living because he'd kept part of himself detached.

He resented that she'd made him "feel," because he'd done a good job of hiding his emotions, but this woman with her knockout figure, perky nose and aura of sadness touched him. He reassured himself he'd have to be a monster not to sympathize with her, but recognizing didn't help. His life worked for him because he didn't allow his emotions to rule him and he'd gotten used to being alone. There was a self-imposed barrier he always kept in place between himself and others.

"I want a family," she said softly, as if confessing an important secret.

He pictured Sabrina with her own family. A complete family, not the one she was planning to have, but a fictionalized version with a stand-up guy for a husband and two kids. One on the husband's shoulders, the other in her arms. Unexpectedly, he felt jealous that he wasn't the stand-up guy with her.

"Isn't there usually a mother and a father in a family?" he asked. He knew he was being a jerk. He should let her be. Give her space and peace. *Don't question her anymore.*

"Yes."

"Why don't you want a husband?" he asked bluntly. He couldn't stop the questions from coming.

"I tried that once and it didn't work."

"Why not try again?"

"Why do you care?" she countered.

All right, lady, show me you have a backbone. ''I think the readers will want to know.''

She wasn't the kind of woman he'd expect to choose to be artificially inseminated. She looked like a lady who'd be more comfortable being married first and then bearing a child. Despite her professional clothing, there was something soft and sweet about Sabrina MacFadden.

''Well, your readers will have to be satisfied with the answers I've given you.''

''Ms. MacFadden, for the amount of money my magazine is spending we expect to delve deep into the heart of you,'' he said.

''The heart?'' she said, fiddling nervously with the heart-shaped charm on her necklace.

Her motions drew his gaze to her smooth, slim neck. He wondered if her skin would be as soft there as on her hand. Probably softer, he acknowledged. Would her floral perfume smell be stronger there? What would she taste like? He shifted back on his seat and stretched his legs to relieve the pressure in his crotch.

Damn.

He leaned forward, ignoring his reaction as best he could. ''Yes, the heart.''

She sighed, picked up her sunglasses and slid them on. The large lenses hid half her face but didn't conceal her as he sensed she wished they did.

''I have bad luck with men.''

How could she? She was the kind of woman most men lusted after. He raised an eyebrow and waited for her to continue. She was hedging—he knew it.

"I'm thirty," she said.

This time there was a hopeful note in her voice, as if maybe he'd buy her answer and let her off the hook. *No way.* Any woman who caused this kind of internal havoc with him was going to have to suffer the same.

"Thirty is not too old to do it the old-fashioned way. How about the truth?" Something about this woman compelled him to delve deeper and deeper. To find out all of her secrets. To peel away the shells she used to protect herself and find her heart.

"I like to be in control. I hate having some man telling me what to do and where to go. And all my married friends don't have that freedom. Plus the men I'm attracted to aren't interested in being fathers."

So, she wasn't ditzy and she had spunk. Each layer he was revealing drew him deeper into her mystery. She was funny, gorgeous and successful, if her classic car was any indication—she didn't need to be inseminated. But she'd made that choice.

He'd started his career as an investigative reporter because he loved solving puzzles and finding the commonality in the most juxtapositioned facts. He liked following a thought to its complicated conclusion and discovering the hidden desires that motivated people. These instincts had served him well while he'd worked the inner-city beat, and for the first time in his job as a life-styles writer he was hungry again, ready to delve, and dig, and expose.

He wanted to take her apart and find out how she ticked. Take away the pieces that were for show, the pieces that kept the world away, and find the true Sabrina MacFadden.

The thought propelled him to his feet. He didn't get involved with "good" women. Sure, he dated, but it was the usual bar-scene-one-night-stand type of woman. Women who wanted a family didn't appeal to him. He was a bachelor and planned on playing the field until he was too old to enjoy sex. Hopefully, into his eighties.

She stood as well. He tossed some bills on the table to cover the check. She pushed a strand of hair behind her ear. Her curls swayed in the wind, and he watched as she gathered the thick mass in one hand.

He wanted her. It was sudden but had been building all afternoon. He wanted to peel away her professional suit and lay her bare on the wood deck of his boat. Nothing but the elements around her. Nothing but him and her, the sun and sea.

But he couldn't have her. Not now, not ever. More than professional ethics played into his decision. More than civilization and the rules of dating and courtship. More than he wanted to admit.

He couldn't have her because she was the kind of woman who wouldn't accept the boundaries he put on relationships. And he knew with gut-deep certainty that she'd push him until she had the response she wanted. *Soft words and demonstrations of affection.*

"Okay, the magazine will take care of getting the paperwork going and I'll see you next week after your consultation," he said.

"Want to meet here again?"

"Sure," he said. He had to get away before he suggested they go home together. Suggested he father a child for her. Suggested they get to the real heart of the matter. Uncover the reason this successful woman peered at him with such vulnerability—and why he wanted to cradle her in his arms and protect her.

"I'll be on time," she said, and walked away.

He watched her hips sway with each step, and despite his uncomfortable arousal, he felt alive in a way that he hadn't in years.

The doctor's office was cold and sterile, even though Monet prints decorated the walls. Nerves and anxious tension settled over her, making her stomach roil. Today was just a preliminary examination, but on her next visit she'd be inseminated. God, she was excited and scared. She was so close to her dream come true.

It was impossible to feel comfortable when you were perched on the edge of a padded table in a paper robe. She glanced around the room, and her gaze fell on the cutaway diagram of a woman's internal organs. Ugh, she didn't need to see what was in there, as long as they worked the way they should.

Lately she'd had doubts about the process, about whether this decision was the right one, especially after meeting Reese Howard a week ago. Never before had she felt an instant attraction to a man. In fact, she'd believed lust at first sight was a myth.

But something about Reese's midnight eyes had

cut straight to her soul. He'd seen past the excuses she'd given everyone else about wanting a baby and forced her to reveal...the *heart*.

He'd demanded it and she'd given it willingly. He was a dangerous man—for her. He asked for things that she'd always wanted to give, answers no one else had been willing to hear. Talking with him had been a joy, really a joy. To share herself and not see that glazed-over look in his eyes had shown her that there was more to men than she'd believed.

Stop thinking about him!

She gazed at a poster of the growth stages of a fetus. Sabrina studied the drawings and her fears started to evaporate. Soon she'd cradle life in her womb. Soon she'd be a part of history, not the written-down kind that was told and retold, but the living kind. The part that survived in spite of politics and social trends. The honest part of life that continued no matter what.

Her doctor entered and after a quick exam told her to change and come into his office. She knew why. There was a lot of insurance paperwork to be done. She dressed quickly and wondered if Reese would be waiting for her. Of course, she knew they'd already planned to meet across the street, but would he show up?

She'd dreamed about him last night, and it had been years since any "real" man had played a part in her dreams. Hollywood heartthrobs had drifted in and out of her dreamscape, but never a man she knew. Reese Howard hadn't drifted quietly through her imagination. He'd forced his way in and taken over completely.

She met Dr. Hyde in his office and filled out the final paperwork. He talked to her again about the process and allayed a few of her fears about what information he'd be giving the magazine. Her medical history was her own, and there was information she didn't want to share. Past mistakes that would bring into question her current decision.

She left his office and hurried across the street. Though it was summer, a cool breeze filled the air, and she tugged her lightweight sweater closer to her body. Quelling the excitement pulsing through her veins, she reminded herself that Reese Howard wouldn't be in her life if she hadn't decided to go to a sperm bank.

He was waiting at the same patio table where they'd sat last time. He wore an aviator-style leather jacket and faded jeans.

"Late again," he said.

Smiling ruefully, she nodded. Punctuality was her cross to bear. She never made it anywhere on time no matter how hard she tried. She'd even set her watch fifteen minutes early for a few months, but that hadn't helped. So she'd stopped wearing one altogether.

He stood and pulled out her chair. The smells of the wind and the sea clung to him. She wanted to somehow get closer to him. To sit on his lap and tell him all her fears and secrets, which she couldn't do.

Because he was going to record her secrets and

then tell them to the world. *You agreed to this,* she reminded herself. Taking a deep breath, she willed away the nervous butterflies, the doubts pounding her like the endless cycle of the waves against the shore, eroding slowly what nature had created at the beginning of time.

Was she fit to be a mother?

He sat with his back to the bay this time, and his sunglasses lay on the table next to his notepad. He didn't look like a reporter, she thought.

"Sorry about being late, again. But Dr. Hyde needed me to fill out a few extra forms this visit."

"For insurance."

"Yes," she said. A waiter approached and Sabrina ordered herbal tea before Reese could order for her. He lifted one eyebrow in question, but she ignored him. The waiter left and she toyed with the ring her parents had given her on her twenty-fifth birthday. A pretty emerald heart set in white gold.

"You seem a little pale," he said.

Damn, she'd hoped he wouldn't notice. "Must be from ordering for myself. All the pressure."

His mouth crinkled, and she thought he'd laugh but he didn't. "Next time I'll order for you."

She'd always enjoyed banter, and now she'd found a safe partner to do it with. And the escape she'd been seeking from her own doubts. "That's okay, I think I better start getting used to it. After all, I'm almost thirty."

He paused, leaned across the table and gestured for her to come closer. She did.

"It might be too late to teach an old dog a new trick," he said softly.

"Who are you calling an old dog?" she demanded.

He laughed out loud this time, and she'd never seen anything more beautiful. Laughter actually changed this man's visage from almost uncivilized to enchanting.

He shrugged. "No one. It's a saying."

"Not a nice one," she said. But she wasn't offended. He'd made her forget her worries for a few minutes. It wasn't her hopes for a baby that woke her up nights in a sweat, but her past. The agreement she'd made with the magazine that sometimes she wished she hadn't.

"So…" He leaned back in his chair, crossed his arms over his well-developed chest and waited.

"So?"

"Why are you pale? Having second thoughts?"

She should have known he'd come back to the heart of the matter. He wasn't the type to give up. Why couldn't he be? This interview process would be so much better if she'd been able to control the reporter. If he'd been the kind of guy she could distract with her legs or a bit of cleavage. Okay, that wasn't the best way to operate, but it worked. Men usually were easily distracted by her looks, but not this guy.

His gaze probed hers, and irrationally she thought he might have read her thoughts. Might have ascertained that she'd been thinking of lying. Don't lie, she thought. Honesty is always better, even when it's painful.

"Second and third and fourth thoughts," she said.

"And?"

"It always comes back to wanting a baby more than anything else."

"Anything?"

She felt his gaze slip over her body and her nerve endings tingled. No, there were other things she wanted. But the baby was the safest thing to discuss with him.

"Yes," she said, and the word sounded weak to her ears.

"More than a man in your life?"

"Yes," she said a little stronger.

"More than—"

"Yes, I want a baby—a family—more than anything else in this world."

"Very well. Then stop having doubts."

"It's not that easy," she said.

His eyes shuttered. "I know."

Sabrina stared at him. She'd taken him at face value and never wondered if anything kept him up at night, if demons crept out from his past and haunted him. But she saw now that they did.

The happy gurgle of a child's laugh drew her attention. A mother and baby walking past the café had stopped. The mother bent double to her child, tied his shoe and tickled the precious, fat little leg. A wave of envy swept through her. She wanted to be that woman so badly her heart felt like it skipped a beat.

Tears stung her eyes before she could cover her face with her hands. She no longer saw the small child in the stroller, but the unborn child she'd miscarried at nineteen. A baby whom she'd wanted badly, but through her own carelessness had lost.

She started to cry in earnest. Reese placed his hands on her shoulders and kneaded deeply, trying in vain to relax her. She had to get away. To escape from the pressure she'd invited by agreeing to these interviews. She'd thought she'd gotten past her guilt and the anger and fear. Obviously she hadn't.

Reese tugged her to her feet, wrapped his arms around her and rocked gently. Why was he doing everything she'd always dreamed a man could do? Why was he fulfilling her fantasies of Mr. Right when she knew he wasn't even close to being that mythical man?

"Don't worry. Fears are natural in first-time mothers. You'll be a great mom."

His words made her feel worse. How could she be? Yet it was what she wanted. It was her secret dream. The one that made her save her money and sit home nights instead of going out with her friends. The one that made her work two jobs and hoard her money like a miser. The one that had shaped who she was so completely that without it she was afraid she wouldn't exist.

"How do you know?" she asked.

"My secretary had the same reactions when she first learned she was pregnant."

"How did she deal with it?"

"That's where a man comes in handy. Her husband distracted her."

"How?" she asked. Reese Howard was a nice man, she thought.

"Well, let's just say she wouldn't give me all the details."

"Oh." She hated the out-of-control feelings coursing through her.

"I have an idea. Why don't we take my boat out on the bay and forget about this story for the afternoon."

It sounded like paradise. And his arms around her felt forbidden. "I don't know."

"Come on. Pretend we're friends."

She didn't want to pretend. She wanted a real friendship with Reese, but knew that could never happen. He had a job to do and *she* was the job. "I don't have any male friends."

"You do now."

A sense of rightness assailed her. For the first time since her parents' deaths she didn't feel alone.

Three

Reese knew there were certain things in life that couldn't be measured. The hours he spent on the *Time Lapse* were one of those things. His thirty-foot sailing yacht was his baby. His car was older and needed a paint job. His house was nice and had a great view of the bay, but he could afford better. His boat was in mint condition. There was no nicer sailing vessel in the marina. He spared no expense when it came to the *Time Lapse*.

The time he spent on the boat worked to counteract the stress of working fourteen-hour days—simply thinking about the boat soothed him. Now that he had left Los Angeles for Sausalito, he spent as much time in the marina and on his yacht as he could spare.

He didn't know what had upset Sabrina. He only knew that he wanted to soothe her. He wanted to bring her closer to him, to bridge the gap she'd put between them when she'd seen the mother and child. He wanted to take her to some place private to explore her depths, and not just for his articles.

He motored out of the marina and headed for the bay. From her seat on the deck Sabrina watched him. Though her large designer glasses covered her eyes, he felt her gaze on him as he steered the boat. When they passed the last buoy and entered the bay, he throttled down and lifted the sails.

The work was hot and the sun burned through the layers of cotton and denim. He wanted to strip naked, to be at one with the elements, but he wasn't alone. And he didn't think the lady would appreciate an elemental male basking in his testosterone.

He removed his shirt and tossed it under his seat. He heard her breath catch and cursed silently. He'd forgotten about the old scars. Not totally forgotten, of course, they were a constant reminder of the past. It was simply that being at sea had lulled him. He pulled his shirt back out and put it on.

He motioned for Sabrina to join him. She moved slowly, as if unsure. Reese couldn't remember a time when he hadn't been at home on the water. He crossed to her and guided her to the steering wheel.

"Reese—"

"Ever been on a boat before?" he asked, cutting her off. He wasn't answering any personal questions. This was his interview. And it was *just* an interview, he reminded himself again. She wasn't a woman he could seduce into his bed, no matter how badly he wanted her there. And he wanted her in his bed very badly.

"No," she said.

Her hair whipped in the wind like living silk. If he leaned closer it would surround him. For a minute he was tempted to do just that.

But reality stopped him. Getting her to relax was one thing, indulging his senses another. Especially since once he lowered his guard she'd jump on him with a slew of questions. Women always did. No woman had ever stayed with him for the long haul. Starting with the death of his mother hours after his birth.

He squinted into the sun and forced his thoughts into the present, back to the lady standing so close to him he could feel the heat from her body.

"Are you relaxing yet?" he asked, leading her further away from the questions he sensed on her tongue.

She shrugged. "I'd be more relaxed if you'd stop interrupting me."

He'd forgotten how spunky she could be. His tonic was working. It had never occurred to her to argue at the café, but here on the ocean she'd found her backbone.

"I know. But there are some things I don't discuss."

"You can leave your shirt off. I was surprised but not bothered."

He was tempted to remove his shirt but knew he wouldn't. Some shames ran too deep and those scars were one of his. In his mind they were as fresh as the day he'd received them.

Looking at Sabrina now, he thought she might feel concern, too. If he removed his shirt and she asked questions in her soft feminine voice, he'd be lured into answering them. And he didn't want to sully the innocence in her eyes by revealing the ugly truth of his past.

"Want to learn how to steer?" he asked.

She sighed. He thought for a moment she wasn't going to let him change the subject, but he could be dog stubborn when he had to.

"Sure."

She pivoted to face the wheel and he stepped up behind her. She had a nice backside. Fully curved and feminine. He wanted to place his hands on her hips and pull her back against his body. But he knew that was foolish. And Reese Howard wasn't a fool.

He placed her hands on the wheel and explained the rudiments of sailing to her. Then he relaxed behind her. The wind and sun played over his skin as he stepped toward her. An attractive woman in his arms, the sea beneath his bare feet, the sun all around him. Another fantasy come to life, thanks to this woman.

"This is great," she said after a few minutes.

He smiled to himself. Finally, the tension eased out of his spine.

After thirty minutes she surrendered the wheel and he piloted them slowly back to the marina. Sabrina hovered next to him while he steered and docked the boat.

She perched nervously on the pilot's chair and removed her sunglasses. She played with the stems. He wondered what was going on in her pretty head.

"I felt like Leonardo DiCaprio in *Titanic*," she said.

Weary but game, he asked, "As if you were going to sink?"

She laughed and he felt better for having amused her. She'd come a long way from the crying woman he'd brought to his sailboat. "No—as if I'm 'king of the world'."

Reese understood completely. There was something about being out in the elements. On the part of the earth that wasn't readily habitable by man and surviving. He loved his boat, had wanted to live on it forever, but none of the women in his life had ever wanted to.

"Is that how you feel?"

"Sometimes," he said.

"Why do you guard every answer?"

"Why do you ask probing questions?"

"I'm telling you the intimate details of my life."

"In return for compensation."

She looked out over the bay. The sun was setting and the breeze was cooler now. She shivered a little, but he suspected it wasn't from the wind. "I feel cheap."

Stay back, he warned himself. Stay away from her. Don't touch.

Yet he moved toward her, anyway. Rubbing her arms with his hands and felt her fragility beneath his grip. He could crush her. How would she ever be able to protect the child she wanted?

"There is nothing cheap about you."

"I'm selling myself for a child."

"You're not. You're sharing yourself with the world for a chance at your dream come true."

She looked up at him, eyes wide, mouth trembling—and he couldn't stop himself. He bent to her, touching her lips lightly with his own. She tasted even better than he'd thought she would. He plunged his fingers into her hair and tilted her head for better access, then took her mouth completely.

Reese blocked out the sun and the sea and the painful memories she'd dredged up. His mouth on hers was sweeter than her first taste of champagne at sixteen and more forbidden. But she longed for more.

His tongue thrust past her lips and teeth and probed the depths of her mouth. Sabrina had never in her life been so thoroughly kissed. She held tightly to his shoulders, covered by his shirt.

She remembered his back and those faded scars. His flesh not movie-star perfect but well-defined— real. Much like the man, a man with facets to be explored. She wanted to touch his skin. To caress each imperfection because it made him seem more human.

Sliding her hands down his back, she slipped them under his shirt. He was warmer than she'd have guessed. *So warm.* The little notch at the small of his back invited her touch and she fingered him gently. Letting her touch expand slowly, she sought out and soothed each brutalized piece of skin. Each part of his back that had been hurt seemingly long ago. She wondered how he'd been injured.

She knew he didn't want to discuss his past. She would have to have been an idiot not to notice the way he kept the conversation away from himself and solely on her, despite his promises that they'd be friends this afternoon and forget about the article. He couldn't forget. It was his job, she reminded herself.

While his mouth moved on hers, she knew it was more than a job to him. Desire pumped through her body. Her blood pooled at her center and her skin felt so sensitized, the slightest touch from Reese sent shock waves through her.

He pulled her closer. At last, she thought. He held her body flush to his and she reveled in it. In the firm, muscled flesh that cradled her softer curves. He was man and she was woman, and on this boat in this time they were the only two in the world.

It had been a long time since Sabrina had stood breast to chest with a man while he kissed her senseless. Too long. She wanted more.

He nibbled little kisses from her mouth to her neck and bit her gently there. Sabrina let herself go. Let herself experience Reese Howard as she'd longed to from the very first moment she saw him.

Weaving her fingers into his hair, she held him to her neck. Felt his own fingers slide under her shirt, then slowly up the front of her body. Feathering a caress along her midriff, then higher, fondling her breasts through the thin layer of her bra. The functional plain white cotton bra that she'd be embarrassed for him to see.

Oh, God, his touch felt so right, so perfect. She wanted more, she needed more. She needed it now.

She leaned into him, and his touch intensified. She slid her hands around to his chest. Rubbing his hard stomach and following the trail of hair that narrowed down his body, disappearing beneath his waistband.

She felt his arousal press the juncture of her thighs and rubbed her body against his. Luxuriating in being woman to his man. In being the elemental answer to his quest. In being the fulfillment of his base needs.

The boat rocked, jarring them apart. Reese grabbed her shoulders to steady her. But Sabrina didn't want him to let go. Her blood was pounding so hard she felt like her heart would leap from her breast.

"That went further than I'd planned," he said, rubbing his hand across his face and through his hair.

She couldn't focus. She could only stare at his mouth. His full, sensual mouth, which she wanted back on her own. Now, she thought.

"It did?" she asked. Her voice was low and raspy, sounding weird to her own ears.

He nodded.

Sabrina thought maybe he was playing with her but realized that their situation was delicate. He could only make the first move for so long. He could only be the aggressor for so long before she'd have to make a decision.

"I..."

"It's okay. I know it went too far."

He gathered up her things and led her to the side of the boat. Sabrina stared at the lonely empty slip next to his—a vacant space waiting to be filled. She thought about her life. About her cold, lonely apartment with its sparse furniture. She remembered her childhood home. The pictures and antique furniture. The Irish linens her mother had collected and her father's classic cars. Her family had had more than the emptiness that plagued her. Her parents had shared intimacy, a life, *everything*.

And this was her last chance.

After she had the child, she wouldn't be able to have a man in her life. Wouldn't be able to make love to a man, sleep with him through the night and wake up to make love again. She'd been celibate a long, long time and that choice had been a smart one.

A girl doesn't forget having to make a tough decision at a young age or the circumstances that led to that decision. But she was a woman now. With a woman's needs and a woman's desires.

She looked into Reese's eyes. Into his darker-than-midnight eyes that made her breath catch in her throat. Into his dark gaze that peeled away layers she'd never let anyone reveal—and she made her decision. Tonight she would be woman to his man.

"Reese?"

"Yes?"

"I don't want to go. I don't think our embrace went far enough."

In response, he pulled her back into his arms, and Sabrina rested there, hearing his strong heartbeat under her cheek and feeling his strength around her. This was the right decision, she thought. *Please, let this be a smart decision.*

Sabrina's apartment looked much like the woman herself, sophisticated and understated. Yet like Sabrina it also held the air of emptiness. A certain sense of expectancy wafted through the open doors. The rooms, which were functional but not lived-in, made his heart ache, even though he'd vowed no woman would ever breach the stone wall behind which he hid his emotions. And he questioned what he was doing here.

The silence felt as heavy as the secrets between them. He had his. They involved more than the scars she'd seen on his back. He knew she had her own secrets, too.

It was evident from the way she'd reacted to the mother and child earlier this afternoon. But those things didn't matter right now. She closed the door quietly behind her. Her wind-blown hair fell in soft waves around her shoulders. Her blouse was rumpled from where he'd had his hands under it earlier, and her long legs were encased in jeans. Blood pooled at the center of his body and his arousal strained against his denim jeans.

He hadn't felt this randy since he'd been a teenage boy experiencing women for the first time. He'd played the game, he reminded himself. He was a lady's man. None of that mattered when faced with Sabrina. Her fresh innocence drew him in ways more experienced women hadn't.

He wanted her in a way that he'd forgotten wanting could be. Sharp, intense and tinged with emotion. He ignored the emotion and focused on the pulse pounding through his body. Demanding he take her to bed. Demanding he mate with her in a primal way. Demanding he move now.

Her pants molded to her perfect thighs and shapely calves. Her lips were still swollen from his kisses but her eyes were clear. Though she wouldn't change her mind, he needed her to say the words aloud.

"Are you sure you want to make love with me?" he asked for his conscience.

"Yes," she said with no hesitation.

His body screamed, *Yeah, baby, let's go for it,* but his mind cautioned him to warn her. She meant more to him than a causal romp. She was the kind of woman who deserved a devoted guy and a wedding. He wasn't that man.

In the back of his mind was the thought that this wasn't the wisest decision. He had to preserve a little distance between himself and Sabrina if he was going to write a decent article. But Sabrina smiled at him from under her lashes in a way that made him want to fall to his knees and crawl to her. She wasn't like the women in his past. She was his dream woman come to life, and he knew he was going to have her.

"It can only be for tonight."

"I know. I want to be with you," she said.

She moved forward and touched his cheek. No one had ever touched him with kindness. He'd been touched in anger and desire but never just kindness. He pushed all concerns about his job and his boss out of his head.

He knew instantly that he'd never be satisfied with just one night. He couldn't wait another minute to touch her skin. To see her spread before him naked and wanting—needing.

He scooped her up in his arms and carried her down a short hallway. Her bedroom was light and airy. The bed was full-size but he wished they were at his place with his king-size bed. However, her bed would do.

He set her on her feet. Sabrina reached for the buttons on his shirt. Reese leaned in and kissed her. Her fingers were quick and nimble as she opened his shirt. She spread her fingers and ran her hands up his chest. He lifted his mouth from hers and gazed down at her.

"Lift your arms," she said.

He obeyed her command.

She smoothed her hands around his waist and to his back. He felt her fingers on the faded scars along the small of his back.

"Sabrina," he said, his voice hoarse.

"Yes."

"Don't touch me there…please."

"No. I want to heal the pain you suffered."

"You can't."

"Yes, I can," she argued while she ducked behind him. She tasted the old wounds with her mouth and tongue.

He shuddered. Reaching behind him, he seized her arm and tugged her back around and bent to taste her mouth again. Using all the carnal knowledge he'd gained after a lifetime of womanizing, he seduced this woman. This special woman with the ability to see past his facade and touch his old wounds.

He peeled away her shirt and bra. Her breasts were full and firm, mostly all nipple. He suckled at the left breast first, feeling her heart pounding furiously. He felt her life pulsing around him and rejoiced in being alive, in being here with her now.

His hands swept down her belly, then unfastened her pants and pushed them out of the way. He straightened, threw back the covers on her bed and positioned her in the center of the mattress. She lay on her back, her wild curly hair spread out on the pillow, making her look like a Playmate centerfold. Her pale body enchanted him. He needed to be closer to her. He needed to be on her, in her, feeling her softness surrounding him.

She parted her legs and he shoved the rest of his clothes off his body in a rush. Bending he retrieved the condom he'd placed in his pocket earlier before they'd left his boat. He needed to feel her heat surrounding him now. He lowered himself carefully on top of her and felt her sigh.

Her hands rubbed along his back, lingering over old wounds and then settling on his buttocks. Her nails scored his flesh as he supported his weight on his arms and rubbed his body over hers.

Her hard nipples rubbed against his chest, her smooth legs cradled his, and her womanly warmth welcomed his hard masculinity.

When he swept his hands down her body and probed at her center, he found her core dewy and ready. Lifting himself away from her, he sheathed his hungry flesh with the condom. He looked into her eyes and watched her face as he penetrated her body.

He watched her eyes widen at the first brush of his hard flesh against hers. Watched her breath catch and hold as he pushed all the way inside her. Watched her bite her bottom lip and felt her hands tighten on his back as he began to thrust.

Keeping his strokes shallow, he waited for her to pick up the rhythm, and when she did, he increased his speed and depth. She wrapped around him like warm, wet, living silk. He couldn't get enough of her. Reaching between their bodies, he caressed the center of her passion. Her body began to clench his and she moaned long and low.

He grabbed her hips, tilted them up and pounded into her until release washed over him. Never had he experienced anything like this before. His climax had never been stronger, strange new feelings floated around him, making him want to pull her closer, to roll over and cradle her in his arms.

Always he'd endured cuddling because he knew women expected it. But this time he wanted to linger. He wanted to stay until morning. He wanted to take her again. And again.

She sighed and snuggled closer to him. Reese rolled to his back and tugged the covers up over them. She kissed him softly on the neck and arousal shot through him.

He caressed his way down her body, needing to feel the warm silk that was Sabrina. The essential Sabrina—elemental woman to his elemental man. He felt not only her body's wetness but the lingering evidence of his passion.

Damn!

He jackknifed into a sitting position and looked down at his body—and the condom, broken.

Four

Sabrina stared at Reese's scarred back as he sat on the edge of the bed cursing like a street thug. He frightened her when he retreated into himself. What had gone wrong? she wondered.

"Reese, what's the matter?"

"Everything. I didn't protect you," he shot back, without turning to face her. The anger in his words was underlined by his body language. He held himself stiffly away from her. She huddled under the sheets, pulling the fabric up to her shoulders.

"Yes, you did," she said, remembering the moment he'd put on the condom. She'd regretted it but knew it was necessary. She'd wanted to feel all of Reese's body caressing hers.

Her familiar bedroom now seemed cold and

lonely. Much as she imagined the Arctic would be on a long, dark winter day—a day without sun. She'd bet everything in her soul on this man, and he was reacting like all the other guys she'd ever met.

"The condom broke."

His words hit her heard, like a punch to the stomach. She couldn't even say it wasn't a good time of the month for her because she'd been taking fertility pills to increase her chances of conception. In fact, she had an appointment next week for her first insemination. It might not be necessary after all, she thought.

She had the insane desire to laugh. But knew if she started, tears would follow, then she'd end up in a ball on the floor clutching her middle.

"Don't worry. It was only one time." Her married friend, Kayla, had tried for six years to get pregnant with her first child.

He stood and faced her. She couldn't keep her eyes on his face. He really was a magnificent-looking man. The sun from the window painted his skin a golden brown. She let her gaze slide farther down his body. He still wanted her, yet she knew he didn't *want* to want her. The way he was pacing she could tell he felt trapped. And she didn't blame him.

"Of course I'm going to worry," he said, jerking up his discarded jeans. He tossed the broken condom in the wastebasket she kept near her dresser. He zipped his pants but left the button unfastened.

She thought about that button. Oh, damn, what had he said? This was important, she reminded herself sternly. *Focus.* Something about worry. "Why? It's not your responsibility."

"So says the woman who wants to be a single mother. Sorry, *babe,* but the game has changed."

She didn't like the way he towered over her as she lay on the bed. Grabbing the sheet, she stood and faced him. He wasn't going to intimidate her. Sabrina MacFadden had learned some hard lessons in her life, and one of them—the most important one—was that she was the only person willing to fight to the death for herself.

She paced over to him and stabbed his muscled chest with her finger. "Nothing has changed, Reese Howard. And don't call me babe."

He leaned down, using his bulk to frighten her. As if he could frighten her after the tender way he'd made love to her. She had to forget about the gentle lover in her bed earlier. This man was a warrior who'd been betrayed. By himself, she realized. His anger wasn't really directed at her.

"The hell it hasn't," he said.

"Don't you cuss at me," she retorted, but the anger had drained out of her.

He cursed again. "I'm sorry."

She sensed he apologized far more than his language. But she gave him the safe answer, in case he wanted a way out. "That's okay. I've heard worse. I work in sales."

Her humor fell flat. Reese's shuttered eyes never left hers, and a coldness emanated from him and spread over her. She rubbed her arms, feeling small and alone.

"That's not what I meant."

"Reese, don't blame yourself. I didn't think about the consequences, either. It was just a mistake."

He glanced up at her, leaning in. He cupped her face with a gentleness she'd never experienced before. "Our lovemaking wasn't your mistake."

"It wasn't?" she whispered, hope springing to life inside her. If it wasn't a mistake then maybe things would work out after all. Maybe he would be her long-haul guy. Because as much as she craved a child, deep down she wanted a complete family.

"No," he said firmly. He kissed her softly. His lips were swollen from their lovemaking. He tasted wonderful. Sabrina thrust her fingers into his hair and held him to her. She wasn't letting go.

He lifted his head and gave her a strong hug. Then he put his hands on her shoulders, separated their bodies at arm's length. "I want you to know, I'll do the right thing."

"What's the right thing?" she asked, fearing that it meant the dutiful thing. The thing guys felt compelled to do when they "knocked up" a girl. But a permanent relationship would require full confession—a husband had a right to know about past medical history that a temporary lover didn't.

He ignored her question, sliding his feet into his boat shoes and picking his shirt up from the floor.

"Reese?"

"Yes?"

"What is the *right thing?*"

"If you're pregnant, I'll marry you."

"Why?"

He paused. "Because if a man seduces a woman—"

"You didn't seduce me."

His eyes glittered like hard diamonds. Dark, rough uncut gems. "Yes, I did, baby. I wanted you and I laid the lure for you."

"You make me sound like some ditzy idiot who has no common sense. You didn't lay a lure for me."

"Yes, I did."

"I'm not going to argue with you. I'm a grown woman responsible for her own actions. And I'm not marrying you because you think we *have to.*"

"We'll see."

Yeah, right, she thought. She wouldn't marry him because of a one-time thing. She'd wanted Reese because he touched something deep inside her that she'd never known existed. She'd wanted to have a chance to be with him before she had a child.

"I'll call you in a few days," he said.

He walked out the door. Sabrina wasn't sure if she wanted to see him again or not.

Reese hesitated outside the clinic's front door. Once again he was reduced to lurking at the sperm bank. He hadn't been sleeping well…too many emotions swirled inside him. He looked up at the sun, letting it blind him.

Unfortunately, it didn't burn through his mind and take away the images of Sabrina. He kept remembering the very first day they'd met, the day they'd sat across the street and she'd confessed she was lonely.

She'd sounded little and lost, as if something precious had been taken from her and she didn't know how to get it back. Never before had he thought of life in those terms. He preferred to ignore the gaping emptiness in his own life. He preferred to ignore the fact that the reckless stunts he pulled didn't fulfill him. He *definitely* planned to ignore the joy he'd felt when he'd held Sabrina in his arms and made love to her.

His soul hungered for her. His heart had cried out—*I'm lonely, too.* But he'd never meant to act on his emotions. Had never meant to acknowledge them. And now duty stood in front of him.

A real man has certain obligations, he reminded himself. His dad hadn't always been an upstanding guy, but one of the lessons he'd beat into Reese was that a real man took care of his mistakes. But was his "maybe-baby" with Sabrina a mistake?

Their lovemaking hadn't felt like a huge judgment error at the time. In fact, no woman had ever touched him on as many levels. She was his teenage fantasy come to life. She was smart and sassy, emotional and tender, and so damned needy that he wasn't the right man for her.

He pushed into the clinic to escape his thoughts. No use chasing his tail until he knew the outcome. Was Sabrina pregnant?

"Can I help you?" the receptionist asked.

The air-conditioning soaked into his skin. The smell of fresh flowers and paper permeated the air.

"Yes, ma'am, I'm Reese Howard. I'm meeting Sabrina MacFadden."

"Miss MacFadden is in the examination room right now. I'll let them know you're here."

Examination room. Just the thought made him queasy. There were some things a man just wasn't meant to know about. He wished he'd waited to meet with her. Wished he'd asked her to meet him at a restaurant or bar. Anywhere but here.

"Mr. Howard?"

He stood.

"Follow me."

He followed the nurse down a long hallway and was seated in a cluttered office. Sabrina stood nervously in the doorway.

"Are you okay?" he asked, getting to his feet.

Her pale face gave the plain white walls color. He'd been loose and free all of his adult life, taking what he wanted and damning the consequences, but seeing Sabrina looking so fragile made him aware that, this time, someone else was suffering for his irresponsibility.

No matter what she'd said he knew he'd seduced her. He knew he was to blame for the outcome of this visit.

"No…yes…"

Reese wanted to close the distance between them and wrap his arm around her. But he knew better. If there was a child, they would marry. He knew this was a shock for her. She'd made a plan for her life. She'd told him all about it and now she was faced with something unexpected.

"It's okay."

She made a soft moan. He put his arm around her despite what common sense dictated. She rested her head against his chest. *Right over his heart.* He felt the muscle begin to beat a little faster. His blood started to flow a little heavier, pooling in his groin.

Dammit, he was trying to be tender, but his body just didn't get the message. Why didn't it? *You're not a respectable kind of guy, Reese. You never will be.* His father's voice from the past sounded loud and clear.

"Excuse me," said a tall, thin man wearing glasses. He entered the room and shut the door behind him.

"Dr. Hyde, this is Reese Howard, the man I mentioned."

"It's a pleasure meeting you, Mr. Howard," he said, offering his hand. "Please sit down."

Reese shook it, though his palm felt clammy. He waited for Sabrina to sit, then seated himself next to her.

"Well, I have some news for you," Dr. Hyde said.

Sabrina's skin flushed, and when Reese tried to meet her gaze she looked at the floor. A knot formed in his gut.

"So, Doc, what's the news?"

"Mr. Howard, it appears you are about to become a father."

"Ah, hell," Reese said. The world slipped away and the burden of duty fell heavy on his shoulders.

Sabrina shot to her feet and dashed from the room

without further comment. Reese realized he'd made a huge error but had no idea how to correct it. The doctor sat grim-faced and expectant. Reese focused on the business aspect first.

"I'll talk to the magazine about reimbursement for any fees they've already incurred."

"That's fine," said Dr. Hyde.

Reese felt the older man's gaze bore into him, accusing him of all the callous things he knew were true. Why did you seduce that girl? Why did you react like a boy instead of a man? Why did you make her leave in tears?

"I'll do right by Sabrina," Reese said, standing to leave.

"She might not let you," Dr. Hyde said.

Reese walked down the long, silent hallway, knowing there was more than a kernel of truth in the doctor's words. Sabrina expected a lot from life and from men or she'd never have made the decision to have a child on her own. And it was going to be tough to convince her to marry any man—even the one who'd fathered her child.

His own mother had died giving birth to him, and Reese knew that he wouldn't be able to find peace in his soul unless he watched over Sabrina. Unless he did everything to ensure that she was safe throughout this pregnancy.

Sabrina's anger carried her to the parking lot and into her car. The classic Mustang was too nice a car to risk driving when she felt out of control. Laying her head on the hot steering wheel, she let her tears roll. She found that crying was the last thing she wanted to do. She wanted to scream at the top of her lungs. She wanted to release her anger in an elemental way.

At the same time, excitement and anxiety warred with her anger at Reese. *She was going to have a baby.* She rested her hands over her abdomen. The small being inside her filled her with all sorts of feelings. Her dream come true and her deepest hidden fear entwined in one.

She needed to get out of here. To get away from the clinic before Reese came out. To escape from the humiliation that coursed through her body faster than ninety-proof whiskey went to her head.

She knew he'd insist on doing his duty. And she'd be tempted to say yes. All she'd ever really wanted was a "real" family. A husband-father to her wife-mother role, and Reese was a man she could see filling the bill. Well, not as he was now. But he had the potential.

She needed more from her husband than cold obligation. If she had to marry she wanted the union to involve all of her emotions. She didn't want to repeat the disaster of her first marriage. In fact, she'd need to be stronger this time to protect her unborn child. She wanted her husband to be overjoyed at the fact they'd conceived a child. She longed for a man who wanted to be a part of her family.

Realistically, she knew her dream wasn't going to happen. The bargain made by two lonely people didn't involve the future. In fact, for once she'd let the future take care of itself. Big mistake, she thought. She'd have to tell Reese about the choice she'd made at eighteen if they became husband and wife.

It can only be for tonight. His words echoed in her mind. She'd agreed. It had been what she wanted as well. Staring into his deep obsidian eyes she'd thought that one night of passion would last her through years of raising a young child on her own.

And if she had her way, she'd still raise her child on her own.

She started the car and drove sedately to her home. The cramped walk-up apartment where she'd shared her body with Reese wasn't the welcoming haven it once had been. She didn't want to be forced to deal with *that* Reese—the man who was so totally different from the Reese she'd sat next to today.

She wanted to hide from the scarred Reese. The one with the open emotional wounds and faded scars. The one who seemed to have something in common with her. The one who hid behind a veneer of sophistication and charm. Granted, it was rough appeal, but it was there.

She sat in front of her building and waited for some reaction to set in. She didn't want to go into her apartment. She'd slept on the sofa since Reese had walked out the door.

A rapping on the window brought her gaze up from her lap. Reese stood there looking like James Dean in his old black-and-white photos. A young tough oddly vulnerable.

She wanted to ignore him. To spitefully lock her door and drive away, but she couldn't. This was the

Reese she feared having to face. The man she felt she could teach to love. The man she wanted to show how to love a woman. Really love her in a way that didn't involve sex. The man with whom she'd created a baby. What a wonderful miracle, she thought.

"Come out," he said.

She set the parking brake, grabbed her purse and opened the door. Reese put his hand under her elbow and led her to the small porch of her building. Sabrina shrugged out of his grip and leaned against the railing. She wasn't going back into that apartment with him. *No way.*

He looked irritated but didn't comment. Propping one shoulder against the side of the building, he watched her from under hooded eyes. Already shocked from his earlier reactions, her nerves snapped.

"What do you want?"

"What do you think?" he countered.

She started to tremble and realized she wasn't up to a sparring match with this man. She doubted she'd ever be able to be his equal here because of her emotions. She cared for him. She wanted his happiness. Even at her own expense? she asked herself.

No, she thought firmly. *I have to think about the baby.*

"Please, tell me why you're here," she said, her anger gone and a tiredness that seemed to come from deep inside spreading through her body.

"I want you to marry me," he said. He seemed sincere.

"I can't," she said, watching him closely for reaction. His mouth tightened and he shoved his hands into his pockets.

"Why not?"

"Because to you it's a duty. Not something you really want."

He paced to the railing next to her and faced the street. "That's not true."

She wished that were the case. "I was in the doctor's office when you got the news, Reese."

"I was shook up. Now that I've had time to think, this is what I want."

"You're sure?"

"Yes," he said with absolute finality.

"I'm not sure."

"What would it take?" he asked, looking her straight in the eye.

Caring, she thought. Some sign of affection. But she could only answer "I don't know."

He watched her and waited. She held her breath and took her courage in her hands, because deep in her heart she wanted to marry this man. Wanted him to share in the joy of parenting a child with her.

"Convince me," she said.

"I know you, Sabrina MacFadden."

She thought of their interviews and how he'd asked for the very heart of her. How she'd given him what he'd asked for and let him see into her soul. She knew now that he was going to use that knowledge to convince her to marry him. And it scared her, yet also elated her. He cared enough to convince her to marry him.

"What do you know about me?" she asked, afraid to believe that he may have seen what so many men in the past never noticed, never bothered to acknowledge.

He leaned closer to her, his chest brushing the arms she had folded under her breasts, his breath caressing her cheek. His words speaking straight into her heart. "You want a family."

She tilted toward him as if he had a gravitational pull that was drawing her. "Yes."

He gripped her wrists and gently separated them from the protective hold on her body. Lifting them, he put her arms around his shoulders and wrapped his own around her waist. "I'm the perfect man to complete your family."

He was so close she saw his pupils dilate as his most masculine flesh nestled into her feminine notch. Desire spiraled through her and she melted.

She touched his cheek with one hand. "Not my family. *Our family.*"

"Our family," he agreed as he bent to kiss her.

Five

Reese reluctantly released Sabrina when she moved out of his embrace. She was like a butterfly or a lightning bug and he wasn't sure in which direction she'd move next. Even though she'd tacitly agreed to marry him, he wanted to hear her say the words.

"Let's go inside and discuss the details," she said.

He followed, hoping after the details were out of the way they could make love again. His body hadn't forgotten the paradise she'd offered that one time. *Only once.* He wanted to make love to her through the night. To turn to her time and again and reaffirm the bond that he'd started to form. The bond he'd cemented with his offer of marriage.

Her apartment was the same as he remembered,

except there were sheets and a blanket on the couch. He lifted one eyebrow at her in question and she blushed. Hurriedly, she scooped up the bedding and tossed it into a closet.

She'd had trouble sleeping, too. Had her dreams been plagued by images of the two of them? Had her thoughts returned time and again to the union of their bodies, which had surpassed anything he'd ever felt before? Or had she simply not wanted to return to the scene of her downfall?

"Have a seat," she said, motioning to the now-bare sofa.

Reese lowered himself to the soft cushions and thought of her curvy body sleeping there the last few nights. She flittered nervously around the room. He watched her pace, wondering if her tension was good for the baby. He'd have to relax her and take care of her. He patted the cushion next to him.

She stared balefully at him for a moment. He felt like a destroyer—a man who created havoc wherever he went. Hadn't life repeated that same lesson time and again? First with the death of his mother hours after his birth and then with the emotional abandonment of his father.

"We're going to be married," he said. It was important that his child have the normal childhood he didn't have. He would do everything in his power to ensure that the small being he'd helped create know safety and security.

Sighing, she crossed the room and perched on the edge of the couch. The flowery scent of her perfume played over his senses like an ocean breeze over his sun-warmed body. Teasing and titillating, it brought to life emotions he'd rather left dormant.

"Okay, let's talk details," she said. She kept her back straight and her tone all business. He wondered if he should offer her a notepad on which to record the fine points of their marriage.

"What do you want to know?"

"What this marriage will entail? Is this a business arrangement?"

"No, why would you think it was?" he asked. From the beginning it had been impossible to treat her with professional distance. If she thought living in each other's pockets would allow her space, she was better at ignoring the truth than he.

"Well, we talked about what I wanted, but I don't think marriage was ever something you desired."

"It wasn't," he said honestly. "Can't a guy change his mind?"

"Maybe a business arrangement would be best. You know I never wanted a husband."

Liar, he thought. She'd wanted a husband but hadn't been able to find that mythical Mr. Right. Reese had sensed from the beginning that there was more to her than the desire for a child. Suddenly it was crystal clear.

"Listen, Sabrina. Maybe I'm not the first candidate most women would think of for a husband, but once I make a commitment I stand by it—for better or worse."

She sighed again and looked down at her lap. He knew that what he was offering went against her own decisions for her life and what she'd said she wanted. But there was another person to consider. Another being that hadn't asked to be born but was going to be just the same. Reese remembered his own childhood and knew that his child needed to have every advantage.

"Listen, honey, you're sweet and caring and everything a child could want in a mother. I'm strong and able and will protect and provide for you and the child. We're the perfect set of parents."

He was banking on her seeing it his way, but what if she didn't? Would he lose the child he'd never met? Would he lose the woman he wasn't sure he wanted to let go of? Would he—

"What about sex?" she asked. Her demeanor was still serious, though she didn't meet his eyes when she asked her question.

"What about it?" he asked. It was one of the perks he could safely enjoy. A long-term sexual relationship was something he'd always craved. The intimacy of the same woman night after night. Yet it had always been outside his grasp. Maybe the child would be the cement he needed.

"Will that be part of our marriage?" she asked.

It was impossible from her tone of voice to tell if that was a perk to her way of thinking or if intimacy was something she'd rather do without. He hoped that she wanted to have sex with him again, because thoughts of her were keeping him up nights.

"Traditionally, it has been."

"Don't be smart, Reese. You're talking about not caring for me. Does sex come with this package?"

He'd hurt her with his blunt rundown of their

skills. But truth now would save her from making false assumptions. "Ah, Sabrina. I care for you as much as I could care for anyone."

"That's not reassuring."

Reese doubted that hearing about his upbringing would bring her comfort, but she had a right to know what she was getting. She had a right to know that the man who'd fathered her child was emotionally deficient.

"Honey, I grew up rough. Like a mangy dog left to wander the streets. My dad died when I was sixteen and I spent the next two years surviving with only my wits. That is why having a family—a real family—is so important to me where this child is concerned. But you need to know up front—I'm not conditioned for caring and affection."

He wished he was, but left those words unsaid. He didn't want to build false hope and was very much afraid he would. The woman standing in front of him was vulnerable. He didn't want to hurt her in any way and was afraid he would. The way he'd been hurt as a child. He was in an untenable position, and the only solution he saw was marriage.

"Were you abused?" she asked, tears sparkling in her deep blue eyes.

He hated talking about the past. He hated pity or sympathy. But he'd brought up the subject. And he honestly felt there were things she needed to know before she made her decision. Marriage wasn't something she'd sought, but it was something he intended to see that she made a commitment to.

"Yes."

"Are you abusive?" she asked.

"No. I'm very controlled. That's why I don't feel emotions."

She leaned back, arms wrapped around her middle, and stared at him. "Can we have more children?"

More children? He didn't want to think about that. He wanted to get hold of the quick fix for this problem and then find smooth waters. "Let's get through this one first. Are we getting married?"

She paused. He felt her slipping away as if this wasn't going to work for her. He needed to convince her. To find some way to make her believe that this was the right choice—the only choice for her and their child.

"Sabrina, I know that life has a way of offering unpleasant surprises along the way. We both know it. But this child doesn't. And our baby shouldn't have to start out slow because he didn't have the advantage of being part of a 'real' family.

"I'm asking you to say yes, for yourself, for me and the child…will you marry me?"

"Yes," she said.

He fought the urge to let out a rebel yell. He hadn't realized how important her agreement would be. But suddenly he realized that if need be, he'd have worn her down until she did agree. "Good," he said, glancing at his watch. "Let's go downtown now and get the paperwork rolling. We can be married in three days."

"Reese, could we have a real ceremony?" she asked in a small, soft voice. A feminine voice that tapped deep into a hidden reserve of longing he hadn't been aware of. A longing to be her Prince Charming—to be her fairy-tale white knight.

He thought of the woman who'd told him her secret dreams in the Bayside Café and how they'd changed drastically for her in the last few days. He thought of all she could have had with an upstanding guy instead of a cold man. And he decided he'd go through the entire wedding circus for her.

"Sure we can. But let's not wait too long."

"Great."

"Why don't you get changed and pack an overnight bag? We'll take the *Time Lapse* out on the bay and celebrate."

"That sounds nice, but I'm not spending the night with you until we're married."

"That's a little like buying a fire extinguisher after your house has burned down, isn't it?"

"It's just how I feel," she said.

"Why?"

She bit her lip and looked away. "We *have* to get married."

Still confused, Reese grasped her chin and urged her to meet his gaze. She did. This was important to her and he wanted to know why.

"Pack a bag just in case. We don't have to have sex just because you spend the night."

"I don't trust myself," she said.

"Then maybe this isn't a wise decision."

"Since we're getting married, I want to wait. I know it sounds silly, but I want to know you a little better before we make love again."

''No problem. I can wait,'' he said.

She didn't respond, just rose to her feet and hurried into the other room to change. Reese felt a ray of hope. Despite the way events had brought him here, their decision might be wise.

Sailing across the smooth bay waters toward the Pacific gave Sabrina the illusion that everything was settled in her world. She liked the feeling, but was pragmatic enough to know it wasn't the case. She knew that despite the fact that Reese wanted intimacy with her, they'd still basically agreed to a business arrangement. And though he wasn't offering her his heart and soul, there was a part of her that was satisfied with their engagement. She'd been raised to believe that a man and a woman expecting a baby should marry.

Because she wasn't a good swimmer, she'd never been a big fan of water, but she felt safe being here with Reese. She realized she'd feel safe with Reese in any circumstances and that warmed her.

Hardly able to believe she was engaged, she looked at her fiancé. Reese stood with his bare feet braced behind the wheel, his face to the sun and his shirt unbuttoned. The tension around Reese's eyes melted away as soon as he piloted the boat out of the marina. She liked watching the change in him. She suspected he did not let many people observe him at his most elemental, challenging himself against nature.

She lusted after him. She'd really said no lovemaking until they were married because she feared he might think she was easy. She wanted his body moving over hers on the bunk below deck. She wanted to caress his chest, visible beneath his open shirt. She wanted to pull his head to hers and let passion take control. But more than that she wanted his respect.

She watched him bring the boat closer to shore and drop anchor. There was a grace in the way he moved. A sureness he felt with himself and his place in the world. A surety she realized she lacked.

Past mistakes shadowed her future, and she knew there were things she should tell Reese now. Today she should bare her soul, let him know she wasn't the sweet girl he thought her to be. She wasn't a perfect lady like her mother had wanted her to be, and her ex-husband had disdained her for that.

Her blood pounded heavily. Her skin felt enervated. The wind served to enhance the feeling. She wanted to throw her arms wide and indulge her senses. But realistically she knew there was no safety in such a course of action.

She had to know more about Reese. Especially since he'd suggested a wedding date in three weeks. She didn't know if she could hold him away from her for that long. He joined her on the long padded bench and sat facing her.

"Tell me about your job," she asked. That seemed the safest line of questioning. When he'd confessed earlier to being abused as a child, she'd wanted to cradle him in her arms. She'd wanted to make up for all the caring he'd never experienced but knew he wouldn't tolerate pity or sympathy.

"Well, you know I'm the features writer for *California Magazine*. Before that I was an investigative reporter for the *Los Angeles Times*."

"Did you always want to be a writer?"

"No, as a child I wanted to be a superhero or a rock star."

"And save the world?" she asked.

"No, just get girls," he said with a laugh.

She smiled to herself, happy to see him relaxed. Maybe they could become friends. That was a safe relationship and would work best in the long run.

"Are you going to get in trouble at work because of me?" She hadn't earlier thought of the possible consequences her pregnancy might cause to his career.

"I don't know. Probably not. I'll reimburse the magazine what they've spent."

Sabrina bit her lip. She knew the expenses would be tough for her to meet, but she should take care of them herself. "I should pay them back. I knew I shouldn't have agreed to let the magazine pay for the procedure."

He glared at her. "I'll take care of it."

"How? I didn't think reporters made lots of money," she said.

"My college roommate is the founder of one of the world's biggest software companies. When he was starting out I loaned him money and he repaid me with stock. I could live off the dividends for the rest of my life."

"Oh," she said, feeling put in her place. But she

wasn't letting him pay back the magazine. That was her responsibility. "Let's not argue. It's my debt."

"It will be *our* debt once we're married, and I'll take care of it," he said with a cunning grin.

"Are you going to be this heavy-footed about everything?" she demanded, not really angry. She was surprised he'd been thinking of them in terms of "us."

"Why?"

"Because if you are, I might push you overboard," she said.

He studied her for a moment. She wondered if he thought she was mentally unstable. But she'd always dealt with confrontations with humor. He leaned closer to her. "Then I'll have to take certain precautions."

"What precautions?"

"Making sure that you need to keep me around," he said in a low husky voice that swept over her rioting senses.

"How?"

"Well, I could try something like this," he said, brushing his lips against her neck. Nibbling gently with his teeth. Oh, man, he made her want to strip naked and offer her body to him. His arm dropped from the back of the bench to her shoulder. He rubbed gently on her back, pulling her closer to him.

Her pulse pounded so loudly, she was sure they could hear it in Asia. His mouth trailed upward from her neck to her cheek and finally brushed softly across her lips. Each stroking of his mouth against hers set off minute contractions low in her belly.

He lifted his head and winked at her. "What do you think?"

"That might not be enough," she said.

"I have other weapons in my arsenal," he said. "Would you like to see them?"

Yes, she thought. Hell, yes. She wanted to see them and experience them. To feel in some way that she'd made the right decision.

She leaned up and kissed him. Taking his mouth as he'd taken hers. Tasting the man and the mystery that was Reese Howard. The boat swayed under them, the sea wind swept around them and Sabrina felt the world melt away.

"Please, show me."

Reese wanted Sabrina more than he craved the relaxation his boat gave him. He knew she felt the same but didn't want her to regret any lovemaking between them before their marriage. He wouldn't actually take her, he thought. He'd give her fulfillment and wait himself for their wedding night. Honoring the wishes she'd expressed earlier. The ones she seemed to have forgotten about.

"Reese?" she murmured. He sipped at her lips. He could spend all day kissing her. Normally he relied on a smooth set of calculated moves when he made love to a woman, but not with Sabrina. Their first mating had been unrestrained. This time he wanted to explore her. To find all of her body's secrets and treasures.

Her hands in his hair held him close, but he kept

the kiss light and teasing. He wanted to stand, then strip, bare her body and take her quickly again.

But he prided himself on his control. He'd learned that passion was the key to destruction a long, long time ago—passion was the dark side of emotion. And he didn't need a refresher course now.

He caressed her midriff and the swelling curves of her breasts, concentrating on the satiny feel of her skin. He brushed her shirt up her arms and over her head and tossed the garment on the hardwood deck. Finally, he was able to taste the smooth flesh he'd revealed.

Her nipples were hard berries pressing against the pale ice-green lace of her bra. He nipped lightly at them with his teeth, then returned to suckle her. The evidence of her stimulation through the lace shot through him.

He reached under her, freeing her feminine bounty from the undergarment. He pushed her back so that she lay on the padded bench next to him; she was more tempting—and forbidden—than the call of the Sirens.

His hands shook with the force of the need coursing through him. He reached out to caress her body, savoring the changing feel of the smooth flesh of her breast, into the velvet softness of her nipple. He tugged and shaped her to his will. Raising her arms above her head, she gave herself up to him. A willing victim to the desire he'd called forth in her.

"Reese, please…"

"Please what?" he asked, massaging both breasts with his hands. She moaned and her cries washed over his skin. Telling him she wanted more. He did, too. He wanted to strip her completely bare and—

"Please taste me again."

Oh, yeah, he thought. His groin hardened even more, and he wondered if he'd be able to do it. To taste all of her and take nothing for himself. Tasting Sabrina was something he'd never tire of. "I'd like to taste all of you."

"Oh, Reese."

He unfastened her shorts and slid them down her long legs, along with her ice-green lace panties that matched the discarded bra. With her arms raised and her long legs moving on the cushions, she looked like a fantasy. His fantasy. His living, breathing dream come to life. The sunlight painted her in soft hues. The sea breeze stirred her hair around her shoulders and raised gooseflesh on her flat belly.

Unable to wait another second, he stroked his way up her legs, covering the curling thatch of hair at the apex of her thighs. Her steamy warmth greeted him, adding fuel to a blaze already out of control.

He parted her and bent to kiss her. To taste the essence of the woman who was going to be his wife. The thought swept through him with a possessiveness he hadn't known he owned. *His wife.* This woman, this tempting creature, was going to be his. It became important to communicate his thoughts in such a way that she'd understand, but wouldn't leave him vulnerable.

She tasted of the elements and of life. He found the center of her pleasure and raked lightly with his teeth until her hips started to lift from the cushions.

When he thrust two of his fingers deep inside her, her flesh clung to him. She clenched him as her cries grew louder, until finally she reached her pinnacle.

He watched her and knew he'd never seen anything more beautiful. His body was hard with want and he took her into his arms. He cradled her next to him, realizing he'd sacrifice anything to keep her safe and happy. He shook as the thought condensed in his mind and the truth shone through.

Though he'd never be able to love her like a husband should, he'd sacrifice himself for this woman and the child she carried in her womb.

Six

Reese hated personal discussions as a rule. He never attended staff meetings and was generally a pain in the butt at work. So he dreaded telling his boss that their interview subject would no longer be artificially inseminated. In fact, he might need to visit his own doctor again because so far, Sausalito had not turned out to be a relaxing cure for his blood pressure.

Jeff was one of the few people he considered a friend. They'd known each other for more than fifteen years. Confessing his error in judgment to a friend was harder than it would have been in L.A. working for a man he just respected.

"What do you mean she's pregnant?" Jeff demanded.

"It happens."

"How?"

"What do you mean *how?* You're married. Go home and ask your wife where those kids of yours came from."

"Funny, Reese. Really funny."

"Don't worry. There is someone else at the clinic who's willing to talk to us. She was inseminated last month and is pregnant now."

"I'm reassured. We should sue that MacFadden woman."

Ah, now we get to the sticky part. "No, we shouldn't."

"Why not?" Jeff asked.

"I'm the father of her child," Reese said.

Jeff released a string of curse words that would've curled a young mother's ears. Reese knew he should have handled the entire matter differently, but at this point he didn't care.

"Want to explain that?"

"No. I'll reimburse the magazine for any expenses. By the way, you're invited to the wedding."

"Do you know what you're doing?"

"Yes," he said. He knew what he was doing—his duty. It was a choice that had been rather simple to make when he analyzed it. Sabrina also touched him in a way he hadn't realized he could be touched. A way he'd always secretly dreamed that a woman would. But he'd never believed he'd find that lady.

The phone rang and Reese glanced at his watch. He was meeting Sabrina in the city at a jewelery store to pick out a ring. The wedding circus had already begun to consume her life, and he hoped to stay far away from the "big top."

"I'll see myself out."

"I want a draft of the first article by the end of the week," Jeff said, picking up the handset.

Outside the office, Reese headed for the elevators. Sabrina stepped out of the elevator when the doors opened. She looked pale but lovely.

"I thought we were meeting downtown," he said.

"I couldn't stand the wait, so my boss offered to let me take an extended lunch. Is everything okay with your editor?"

He was touched by her concern but knew it was more than that. She'd wanted to take care of the details of her arrangement with the magazine. He directed her back into the elevator and hit the down button. "Yes."

Nervously, she toyed with the strap of her handbag. "I thought if he had any questions I could tell him it was all my fault," she said.

He realized he was responsible for those feelings. For her being scared and nervous. Dammit, when was he going to stop living up to the old man's predictions? The words that had poured from his bitter father's mouth every time he'd had to "discipline" Reese for not living up to his expectations of a man.

"Don't worry, everything is fine," he said to reassure her. But how could he? He couldn't say he'd make everything okay because being a husband and father was something he had no idea how to do.

"Are you sure?" she asked. It was as if she'd seen into his soul and glimpsed his doubts.

"I just said so, didn't I?" he snapped.

She stiffened and moved away from him. She didn't need to. No one was more shocked than he was. Never had his temper slipped its control before, even by that tiniest bit. It had to be the situation. Feeling like a failure, here at work, the one place he'd always been successful.

"Sorry," he muttered.

The doors to the elevator opened, but to his surprise Sabrina didn't rush out.

"Are you okay?" she asked.

He nodded. What was he going to say? He'd lost control. It wasn't something that had happened before and he didn't anticipate it happening again. He couldn't let himself get involved with this woman emotionally. He couldn't let her slip any farther past his guard because already she was in dangerous waters. And she was pushing *him* into uncharted waters.

"Let's go buy our rings," he said.

"I'll drive. That way you won't lose your parking spot. Unless that will offend your masculine pride."

"Of course not, I've always wanted a chauffeur," he said, trying to be light when he felt like doom.

Are you abusive? Her question from days ago echoed in his mind. She didn't want to be saddled with a man who couldn't control himself. Reese knew from experience just how dangerous that could be. Especially for a child. A child wouldn't understand why everyone else had a safe home and he lived in a battle zone.

Her car was steamy after sitting in the afternoon sun. She put the top down and climbed behind the wheel. Reese hesitated before getting into the car. It wasn't that he didn't trust himself. Something more needed to be said and he had no idea what to say.

"Get in," she said softly.

He sat next to her. The scent of her perfume flowed around him, soothing the emotions that were boiling inside him. Resting her hand lightly on his thigh, she studied him.

He met her gaze. She didn't have her sunglasses on and her eyes were wide and sincere.

"Snapping at me doesn't make you abusive."

"I know." Though, deep inside he didn't. Verbal abuse was still abuse. He wouldn't let her find any more weaknesses in him.

She sighed, then picked up her sunglasses and slid them on. "I was being annoying."

"You were?"

"Yes."

"Intentionally?"

"Well, yes. I wanted to take care of the matter at the paper myself even though you insisted."

"It's a man's job—"

"Reese, nothing is a man's job anymore."

"Some things still should be."

"Name one."

Taking care of his mate, he thought. But didn't say it out loud. She gave up waiting and navigated the car out of the parking lot and into the lunch-hour traffic. Her words rang in his ears and he knew she was right. In today's world there were no gender-specific jobs, but it didn't mean society was right. He acknowledged that a lot of things would be changing in his life with this marriage.

The jewelry store had been crowded, but they were shown to a private room and had their choice of trays of rings brought to them. Reese hadn't been kidding when he'd said he had money. He shelled out more for the rings than she'd have expected for a man doing only his duty. It underlined to her the seriousness of Reese's intentions toward her.

The wedding set they'd chosen hadn't needed to be sized, and after they'd paid for the rings, Reese had pocketed the little velvet box that held her engagement ring. They walked to the car in silence. The heat of the day wrapped around them.

"Why don't you call your boss and see if you can get the afternoon off?" Reese asked.

"I can't. I have a presentation to finish before five. As a matter of fact, I'll be working late tonight."

"Why did he let you go earlier?"

"I was making him crazy pacing around the office."

"Pull off over here. This will just take a minute."

Sabrina pulled into a spot close to the park that overlooked the bay. Reese came around to open her door for her. She liked that little courtesy that he always offered her even if it was old-fashioned.

He directed her to a sun-warmed bench. The

breeze blew across her cheeks and she closed her eyes, turning her face toward the sun. It was a good day, she thought.

"I love the sea," Reese said as he sat next to her on the bench. "I always have."

Sabrina thought she knew why. The craving of water had always been symbolic of the craving for love. And if ever there was a man who lived in the desert of life it was Reese Howard.

"I'm not a big fan of water."

"Why not?"

"I can't swim. Well, not really well. I almost drowned as a child."

"I'll teach you."

"Okay," she said, though she doubted she'd be able to pay attention to any lesson he offered while he was clad only in swim trunks.

He cleared his throat and then stood. Sabrina's heart leapt to her throat. She nervously twisted the ring her parents had given her around on her finger.

"Sabrina," he began, then looked out to the water.

"Yes," she said.

He pivoted back to face her, then dropped to one knee, pulling out the velvet box he'd pocketed. "Will you marry me?"

She smiled at him through the tears that stung her eyes. Here he was being her prince again though she knew he'd deny it. Here he was making her rejoice in the fact that she'd met him and made love with him. Here he was making it so easy for her to fall in love with him even though she knew it wasn't wise.

"Yes," she said, her voice cracking with the emotion she hoped to hide from him.

He slid the engagement ring on her finger and held her hand tightly. He made her feel safe in a way she'd never experienced before. She hoped she'd be able to offer the same security to him.

He kissed the back of her hand with old-fashioned gallantry that she would have sworn men had forgotten long ago. He wasn't a lily-white, never-fought-a-battle city boy; her Reese was a hardened warrior who also knew the value of the softer things in life. He knew the value because he'd hardly ever found those things. It was her duty, she decided, to give him those things.

He stood and pulled her to her feet. She nestled close to his chest, embracing him for all she was worth. He bent and brushed a petal-soft kiss against her forehead, then her eyes and cheeks. Finally she tilted her own head and found his lips with her own.

His taste was heaven and she drank from his mouth like a parched woman drinks water. The kiss turned carnal with a thrust of his tongue and she moved closer, craving him more than she'd ever believed possible.

He pulled back after long minutes had passed and she stared up into his eyes.

"Thank you," she said.

"No, thank you for the honor. I'll try to live up to your trust."

"I'll do the same," she said, and knew that she

needed to tell him more of the details of her past. She needed to do it now before the wait was too long and the truth she held in her heart became a lie of omission.

Instead of a bachelorette party, Sabrina's friends held a get-together the night before the wedding. Reese was as close to being relaxed as she'd ever seen him, and though he didn't appear ecstatic, he did smile easily. Sabrina had suggested an outdoor wedding, which appealed to Reese. He'd said that only when he was outside did he truly feel comfortable and free. But the church wouldn't perform an outdoor ceremony so they were being married in a small chapel.

She wanted him to be happy with this marriage. The one he'd pushed for. Sometimes when they were together it was as if he held himself apart. She hoped their wedding would bridge that gap.

She'd planned a nice, stylish wedding but not overly ostentatious. After all, this was her second time around. She prayed this marriage would be a success, unlike her marriage to Scott. She should pull Reese aside and tell him about that marriage now before it was too late. If she waited too long to tell him about her first pregnancy and the choice she'd made then, he might think she'd betrayed him. Trust was so hard-won from Reese. She doubted he'd ever fully trust another person, but she wanted him to trust her. If not for her sake, then for their child's.

The house was filled with Reese's friends from

work and the people who Sabrina counted close. Her best friend, Kayla, and her husband, Larry, were hosting. She watched Reese talking to one of the guys he'd invited. He was at ease with himself, and Sabrina wondered if he'd ever be at ease with her. She didn't expect them to become twins or soul mates, but she envied the ease he had with others.

Despite the air-conditioned room, she was hot. Taking a healthy sip of her tonic water, she wished for something stronger. She'd thought about single motherhood but hadn't considered getting married because she had to. Marriage was another ball of wax and one she wasn't sure she was prepared for. But only selfish reasons would keep her from marrying Reese. She'd been raised to take responsibility for her actions and meant to do so now. Besides there was something about Reese, something wonderful, that made her warm inside, and she'd never experienced those feelings before.

"Why are you hiding in the corner?" Kayla asked out of the side of her mouth. It was her imitation of a spy making subtle conversation. They'd played the scene a number of times in the past. Sabrina felt a rush of gratitude and affection for her best friend.

"Well, Bond, I'm not hiding," Sabrina said, answering the same way.

"I like Reese," Kayla said.

Sabrina made a face at her best friend. "I think I'm going to have a nervous breakdown."

"No, you're not. Every bride is apprehensive."

Sabrina realized that there was much she didn't know about weddings. At eighteen, for her first wedding, she'd left every detail to her mother and had been just a player in the event. But this time she'd made herself and Reese the most important players. And she had more at stake, she acknowledged. More to lose if this didn't work out. Reese already meant more to her than Scott ever had.

"I wasn't apprehensive when I married Scott."

"That should reassure you," Kayla said dryly. She'd always hated Sabrina's husband and thought he was too self-centered. It had turned out she was right.

Sabrina laughed. "Thank you."

"No problem."

Her best friend looked like a cover model. Tall, slender, she wore a Donna Karan pants suit with the same ease most women wore jeans and a T-shirt. Under that sophistication was the person who knew her best. Who'd seen her at her lowest and helped her through it.

"I hope this isn't another mistake," Sabrina mused.

"How could it be? Reese is ten times more man than Scott."

"Yes, you're right."

"Come on, let's go head Larry off before he scares Reese away."

Sabrina watched the men as she followed Kayla across the room. Reese was taller than Larry, and to her eyes more attractive. Reese glanced up when she approached, and put his arm around her when she was within his reach. His touch at her waist and hip felt right. Some of her fear eased.

What would Reese think when he saw her to-morrow? Would something magical happen to transform a matter of duty into love?

Don't try to make the situation into something other than it is. He can't love you. And you don't need love.

But her heart argued. Any man as tender a lover as Reese *could* care, maybe even love. But was she willing to take the risk of her own heart? He'd honored her wishes not to make love again until their wedding night. But Sabrina admitted to herself that she would have backed down on that front. She wanted Reese with a surprising passion. He was the only man she'd ever met who could make her forget the control she'd craved so desperately in her life.

Larry and Kayla moved on and Reese maneuvered them into a quiet corner. "I like your friends."

"They like you, too."

He smiled. One of his little half smiles that he substituted for the real thing.

"How are you feeling tonight?" he asked.

"Fine," she said. He'd been very concerned when he'd stopped by this morning after her first bout of morning sickness. The real thing was quite different than she'd been led to expect from reading books on pregnancy.

"You look *fine*," he said with a devilish grin.

She thought he was teasing again, but a certain light twinkled in his eyes. He brushed his lips against hers, teasing her mouth by running his tongue along the length of her lower lip. When she gasped, he slid his tongue inside her mouth. He tasted of Scotch and soda and something elemental that she only associated with Reese.

His body pressed to hers felt warm and solid. She held him close and savored his warmth. She'd been cold and lonely for a long time, and suddenly she wasn't anymore. Standing there in the shadows with Reese pressed against her, Sabrina realized she was committed to this man. And committed to making their life together successful.

"Mmm, you taste good. Open up, honey, and let me have another sip."

"Reese, we're in a crowded room."

"We're engaged, I'm sure they'll understand," he said, nibbling at her neck.

Shivers of desire raced through her body and pooled at her center. A new excitement sang in her veins. She understood that this man was her mate on a number of levels.

They'd make a good marriage.

Reese straightened his bow tie and thrust his hands into his pockets. A quick glance at his watch confirmed that the wedding would begin in less than thirty minutes.

"Nervous?" Jeff asked.

"Me?"

"Yeah, macho man, *you.*"

Reese shrugged. By nature he wasn't a nervous person, so he refused to classify his feelings as nerves. He'd rappelled a glacier in the dead of winter and come back alive. Getting married should be a piece of cake.

"I've never been more scared than when Stella and I were married," Jeff said quietly.

Bare emotion made him itch, as if his skin were too tight. He wanted to ignore Jeff but knew exactly what his friend was driving at. "When did it change?"

"When I saw her walking down the aisle on her dad's arm. Her face lit up like she'd just seen something precious and rare, and I knew I'd made the right choice."

Sabrina didn't have a father to give her away so she was walking herself down the aisle. They were both alone in the world, he thought.

"Yeah?"

Jeff landed a playful punch on Reese's shoulder. "Yeah, man."

The minister came in, saving Reese from making any comment. He couldn't imagine seeing any expression on Sabrina's face that would make a difference. He knew that his fears stemmed from childhood and his past. He'd never made a commitment to a woman that had lasted longer than two months.

What was he doing? Here he was signing on for the long haul with a woman he'd known even less than two months. And their commitment would go on for the rest of their lives. They'd created a child together. They'd forged a bond neither of them had expected.

"Ready, son?" the minister asked.

Hell no, Reese thought, but he nodded at the older

man then looked around the small Episcopal chapel. It was intimate and charming. Much like the woman who'd shortly be his wife.

His wife, Reese thought. It was the one thing he'd thought never to call his. *A wife.* The soft, feminine person who helped make a cold, stark house into a home. The sweet, caring person who'd wrap a child in a warm blanket on a cold night and hold the precious bundle close. A warm and willing woman who'd fill the empty part of his hungry soul.

As much as he wanted to believe Sabrina wasn't the answer to his secret dreams, he wasn't sure. How could he protect her and not hurt himself?

The answer was in limiting the time he spent with her. To limiting the couplings they had together. That, more than anything else, had sustained him through the long weeks of their engagement. By nature he wasn't a celibate man. But he'd wanted to test his control and he had succeeded.

He knew that when Sabrina swelled big with his child, his own possessiveness would grow, as would the need to claim her in the most elemental way. He'd already felt the urge to do so and they weren't even married.

He took his place at the front of the small church, watching down the candlelit aisle for his bride.

His bride.

The words echoed in his head like the promise of ice cream to a small child. But he wasn't a child anymore. He was a man who knew that sometimes the very thing you'd hoped for turned out to be a big disappointment. He knew some wishes left you open for the biggest hurt of your life. He knew that he'd forgotten how to hope a long time ago.

Reese reminded himself that he was too old to relearn the lessons life had taught him.

Music sounded through the small chapel and the procession began. Jeff nudged him and motioned with his head to the back of the church. He scanned the shadows for Sabrina, then saw the faint traces of her creamy dress behind the simple design of the maid of honor's navy dress.

Finally, the children and the bridesmaids stood at the altar and the wedding march began. Sabrina emerged from the shadows like a butterfly from a cocoon. Radiant and breathtaking. Full of light and life. His heart constricted in his chest. And Reese forgot to breathe.

She was radiant. She was the light he'd needed for so long to fill the darkness he lived in. But he knew without a doubt that the shadows of his past could easily turn her light into darkness. Making life better for his unborn child was a noble cause and one that he'd dedicate his own life to, but ruining this sweet woman was something he'd have to guard against.

Her satin dress was simple yet elegant, a straight sheath that had none of the embellishments of most wedding gowns. Her reddish-brown hair added the only color in her ensemble. The contrast of her fiery hair against the purity of her dress touched him. It spoke starkly of the woman coming to him. The woman who was both a sweet innocent and a fiery temptress.

Sabrina came right to him with no hesitancy in her steps and placed her hand in his. He helped her up the steps. Her hand was cold and he wondered if she, too, had doubts.

"Okay?" he whispered under his breath.

She nodded and smiled up at him. Her Caribbean-blue eyes sparkled up at him through the veil. He wanted to taste the smile on her face. To consume some of the happiness he saw there. To swallow the same rainbow she had so that he could glow within.

"You?" she whispered.

He nodded.

The minister began the service, and as they stood together at the front of the church, a peace like he'd never known assailed him. It was the kind of peace he'd thought never to have. Holding Sabrina's small hand in his, he was struck by the differences between them.

They were two together now. They were two strangers who'd been alone in the world and were coming together to make three. To make a family.

Reese tried to let the happiness of the moment play in his soul, but part of him knew that not all families were happy. Not all mothers and fathers stayed married. Sometimes the mother was stolen away in a careless moment. And sometimes the innocents were the ones who were hurt the deepest.

Seven

The rush of emotions that had swamped her during the wedding and reception fled Sabrina as she stood in the marble bathroom of the honeymoon suite. The understated elegance and opulence of the hotel overwhelmed her, but not as much as the realization that her new husband moved comfortably through this world. Everyone she knew lived pretty much paycheck-to-paycheck. That there were people in this world who didn't was an anomaly.

A forceful rap on the bathroom door brought her out of her unhappy comparisons.

"Planning to come out tonight?" Reese asked. His voice, though muffled by the heavy oak door, shivered through her. She liked the way he made her feel, as if she were the only woman in the world for him.

"I'll be right out."

"I ordered a bottle of Dom Pérignon from room service."

"Hey, I'm pregnant."

"I know. But a sip won't hurt."

Who knew if that was true? Sabrina wasn't going to chance it. And at the urging of her first husband, she'd taken a calculated risk with her first pregnancy, and look how it ended.

If this marriage had any chance of surviving, it depended heavily on the baby growing in her womb. The baby she'd sacrificed so much to have. More than she'd ever imagined sacrificing. She should confess to Reese about her first pregnancy tonight, except she was feeling cowardly.

She wanted to enjoy her wedding night with Reese, and she knew that ugly confessions would ruin everything. She wanted this night, their first night as man and wife, to be beautiful. Tonight was not the time to expose her flaws. Maybe later after they were friends, she'd feel better about telling him.

"Come on, honey."

He sounded tender and sweet. She didn't know if she'd ever come out of the bathroom. Though the woman reflected in the mirror looked sexy and sophisticated, Sabrina felt like an awkward girl. An average woman who had no right to be in this designer peignoir in the fancy honeymoon suite. A woman who didn't deserved to be here with Reese Howard.

"If you won't come out, I'm coming in."

Sabrina sighed and reached for the door. She paused, realizing suddenly the reason for her shyness. She was hiding. Not from Reese or his money and sophistication but from herself. She felt very vulnerable tonight.

The doorknob turned slowly and Reese entered the bathroom. She'd left only the light over the garden tub lit. He looked breathtakingly handsome in the low lighting, wearing only a pair of faded denim jeans that were unfastened but zipped.

He sat next to her on the edge of the tub. Her hands began to shake as his body heat wafted toward her. Unconsciously she leaned forward, wanting to give up the burden of her undeclared secret and share it with him.

Once he knew, he could share the weight of her past. There were things she'd have to tell him. Things that he'd probably find out sooner or later, such as her irresponsible teenage years. And the major mistake in judgment she'd made at nineteen.

"I'm sorry," she said softly. There was nothing else to say. Her confession would have to wait. She couldn't tell him tonight. Not after the roller-coaster day she'd had. She would have bet the Mustang that he would have backed out at the last minute. But he hadn't. Nothing meant more to her than the expression on his face as she'd walked down the aisle toward him.

"For?"

"Hiding."

"It's not every day that a woman gets married," he said.

"I was married before." She wanted to unburden herself at least partially, and if he knew she'd been married it would make certain truths easier for him to accept later on.

"I know," he answered quietly. The lamplight played over his muscled chest and she wanted to bury her fingers in the hair there.

His answer sank in. "How?"

"You told me at the first interview." Wrapping an arm around her, he pulled her into the curve of his body. He felt like home. He felt like everything she'd been secretly searching for but had been afraid to find. His body was heaven next to hers, and she felt her blood surge and pool at her center.

"Were you ever married before?"

"No."

"Why not?" she asked, knowing she was buying time, but genuinely interested in learning more about him.

He leaned forward, bracing his forearms on his thighs. "With my upbringing and all, it didn't seem a wise choice."

"How bad was your upbringing?" she asked, thinking there might be a connection between the scars on his back and the abuse he'd suffered at his father's hands.

"Well, you've seen my back."

"Yes," she said, reaching out to caress him. He was warm and solid beneath her fingers and seemed invincible. Now she knew why. He'd had to be strong to survive. Suddenly, Sabrina was fiercely grateful for her battered warrior husband.

He was the type of man who'd fight to the death for her and their child. He'd protect them even at the cost of his own life. Something her ex-husband would never have done.

She looked at the emotions she couldn't read in his eyes, and though she wanted to know more about him and the past, she sensed that tonight—this moment wasn't the time.

"I'm ready to stop hiding," she said. Her voice sounded low and raspy to her ears.

"Good." Reese stood and lifted her into his arms. She'd always wondered how Scarlett had felt when Rhett had carried her up that staircase and now she knew. She felt like a princess who'd just been awakened by her prince.

Reese wasn't a romantic guy, but he'd been single long enough to have picked up some useful knowledge about seducing a woman. He felt a little cold-hearted using his knowledge on Sabrina, but he wanted their wedding night to live forever in her memory. He'd lit scented candles around the room, sprinkled rose petals on the sheets and even hauled out his old volume of Lord Byron's poetry.

But when he looked down into her heart-shaped face and saw her dreams in her eyes, he couldn't be cold and calculated. He set her in the center of the bed and propped pillows behind her.

He'd pressured her into marrying him, but there

was no recrimination in her eyes. She wanted to be here. *With him.*

He poured champagne into the two fluted Waterford glasses, filling one with barely a thumbful for Sabrina. He knew pregnant women weren't supposed to drink, but a sip wouldn't hurt her.

"A toast to our marriage," he said, handing her the smaller portion.

"Life, love and happiness," she said as she lifted her glass.

Reese couldn't drink to that. He didn't believe in love—and he didn't want Sabrina to believe in it, either. It was dangerous to believe in things that would never come true.

"Long life and happiness," he said, lightly touching the rim of his glass to hers.

The glow of joy in her eyes dimmed a little. She barely touched her tongue to the small amount of champagne he'd poured in her cup. Reese swallowed with a lack of finesse that he found unnerving.

He felt the shackles of youth pulling him away from the man he'd become and back to the rough boy he'd been. He couldn't be that boy here with Sabrina, yet she called to the wildness in him as no other woman ever had.

He took her glass and set it aside along with his own. While the jazz saxophone of Kenny G filled the room, he stood to watch his bride. To watch the woman who'd become his in front of God and man. The woman who now would cleave only to him.

He wanted her. His jeans were painfully tight and his hands trembled with the remembrance of her sat-

iny skin under his touch. He wanted to peel away
the peignoir she wore to tempt him—no garment
could tempt him more than her womanly body.

He reached for the thin strap of her nightgown
and pulled the left side down her arm, baring her
breast. The soft fabric cupped her flesh as he longed
to. Reese leaned forward and stroked her nipple with
his finger and felt her body change, readying itself
for him.

He craved the release to be found in her sweet
body, the way he'd once craved normalcy and de-
cency. She shivered and moved restlessly on the
bed.

"Like that?"

She bit her lip and nodded. Her hesitancy made
him remember the first time they'd made love and
he'd seduced her. He wanted to know that she was
willing.

"I've been a good boy and waited as you asked,"
he said, more to himself than to her.

"Then come collect your reward," she said. Her
brazen words surprised him. He saw her approving
gaze slip down his body. He wished her hands
would take the same path. His arousal strained
harder against his zipper.

"Woman, you're undoing me," he said.

"Good," she said with a sexy laugh.

"Undress for me, Sabrina. Let me know that there
is no seduction going on this time."

"Yes," she said. She pulled her peignoir over her
head and flung it on the floor at his feet. She lay
back against the cream-colored sheets, her body

flush with desire and her reddish-brown hair a splash of color so intense that it made him believe in dreams again. He forced the thought away, pushed it under the wall where he hid anything that could hurt him. Instead he focused on the blood running hotly in his veins and the woman spread before him like a luscious feast.

He shed his jeans hastily and walked toward her. She boldly stared at him. And when he was within reach, she touched him. It was a soft caress like a butterfly landing on a flower, barely disturbing the beauty of the petals. He felt life surge within him. Felt all of his power as a male narrow down to this one instant.

''You are so beautiful,'' she said softly. She sat up and leaned forward, brushing gentle kisses against the heat of him. Her hair brushed his thighs, and Reese wanted to thrust his hands into her hair and hold her to him.

He needed to give her the same pleasure she was giving him before his control deserted him. He nudged her back against the pillows. She stared up at him with a hot look that would have broken a weaker man. But tonight Reese was in control and he meant to stay that way.

Framing her neck with his hands, he swept them down her body. Caressing her desire-hardened nipples. Unable to resist, he bent and suckled her. He drew on her until her hips started to shift on the bed and her nails scored his back. Moving to the other breast he treated it to the same attention.

He smoothed his hand down her flat stomach, rubbing a small circle over the spot where his tiny child lay. Then he moved lower to the nest of curls that guarded all of her feminine secrets.

Her legs moved restlessly against the sheets. Reese teased her with a circling caress, intentionally avoiding the one spot he knew she most wanted his touch.

"Reese," she said urgently.

"Yes?"

"Please…"

He parted her soft flesh and felt the warmth of her welcome. Felt the rush of feminine acceptance of him and who he was. Felt as if he'd finally been brought to the gates of heaven. He caressed her until her hips writhed and her moans grew louder.

"Now, Reese."

He slid up over her, guiding his body to her humid hearth. God, he wanted her. Sensation tingled along his spine and she smiled up at him with such sweet splendor as he thrust into her.

He held on to his control. He reached between their bodies to caress the center of her passion, and as she convulsed around his flesh and trembled in his arms, he let himself follow her.

Falling down from a high like he'd never known, Reese wondered how he was going to protect the walls that he knew needed to stay in place. There was no way to keep himself away from her physically. He'd have to retreat emotionally.

The Dave Matthews Band played loudly in the background as Sabrina carried another box of her belongings into Reese's house. She'd been pleased to realize that they shared similar taste in music, but there were still so many areas where her new husband was a stranger.

His house was a large property that sat on Mount Tam and overlooked San Francisco Bay. It had been three weeks since their wedding night when Reese had set her soul and body on fire and then retreated with all the finesse of a man accustomed to hiding himself.

The rational part of her mind knew he was doing nothing more than he'd said he would when they'd talked about their marriage, but part of her—the emotional, sappy part—hated the distance.

She'd been slowly moving into his house, and today she'd brought the last of her possessions. Reese had suggested they live on the boat, but Sabrina had put her foot down. She wanted to be able to move around, and she was sure once he'd thought about it that he would have retracted the offer. Reese wanted distance between them. On the confines of a thirty-foot yacht there wasn't that much room.

The house was large and of better quality than even her childhood home. She'd married up without even trying, she thought wryly. But she'd trade all of her husband's monetary worth for one warm, genuine smile and an embrace outside of the bedroom.

She set her box on the Mexican tile in the foyer. Most of her stuff was cheap and junky compared to Reese's, but she loved her tacky little knickknacks and prints. Would he suggest she hide it away somewhere?

She had a vision of a pile of boxes in his garage with the words Sabrina's Junk written on the side.

"Where do you want this box?" Reese asked.

Sabrina glanced at him. He wore faded cutoffs and no shirt. Sweat glistened in his chest hair and she wanted to reach out and touch it, to capture the essence of Reese on her finger and taste it.

"Sabrina, the box?"

Most of the rooms were full of her boxes. "I don't know. Is it labeled?"

"Nope," he said.

She knew he was thinking that he wouldn't have asked if it had been. She was turned on by looking at her new husband, but she wanted their relationship to be more than sex. "Sorry. Just dump it here and I'll open it up later."

"I'll put it in the spare room. Then you can leave it if you're too tired to get to it today."

"Thanks," she said. He was always so solicitous when he thought she might be feeling the effects of her pregnancy. Which she admitted she was. On television and in the movies women looked lit from within when they were pregnant.

Sabrina didn't feel all aglow. She was excited at the thought of having the child and holding the baby in her arms, but the actual birth process scared her. She was also afraid she might do something wrong and lose the baby.

Physically, she was tired and her skin felt tight. And the pressure of not confessing her past weighed heavily on her. She also felt too old to be having her first child. She knew a lot of women were waiting until they were in their thirties to have kids, but it didn't help her attitude.

She felt old, tired and fat, and when Reese looked at her, she tried to hide her feelings but knew she hadn't. Her boss had told her once that her feelings were always revealed on her face. And as much as she tried to hide her emotions, she never could.

"Let me store this box upstairs. Why don't you go out on the porch and I'll bring you some lemonade?"

"You don't have to baby me, Reese."

He shrugged. "I'm not."

She smiled gently at him because she knew he hated the softer feelings she aroused in him. At first she thought he felt nothing for her aside from lust and duty, but it was becoming more and more apparent that he felt too much and tried to hide those things. "You are a sweet man, Reese Howard."

"There's hardly a sweet bone in my body, Sabrina. One of the things we agreed to in this marriage was that I would take care of you."

She didn't remember agreeing to that. But she was flattered by his concern. "Is this like when you decided to pay my bills at your magazine?"

"Yes," he said with a devilish grin. "If you argue with me you won't win."

"Maybe I'll just wait and get even with you later while you're asleep."

He gave her a sexy look and sparks of desire shot through her. Her tender nipples hardened. His gaze swept down her torso, lingering, it seemed, on her breasts.

"A man can only hope."

She laughed as he headed upstairs to the spare room. The love she felt for Reese deepened as he helped her through her bad moods. He didn't have to. He could have dumped the box and walked out the door, but he'd stayed.

Her heart felt lighter with the hope that he was beginning to fall in love with her. No matter what he'd said about not being able to love, she knew that every human could love. Reese simply hadn't had anyone shower affection on him and didn't realize he had a deep well of caring inside of him.

As his wife it was her duty—no, honor—to show him. To make up for the cold days of his past. His childhood had shaped him into a hard man who'd never expected success, but he'd achieved it and she was proud of him for it.

He came back down the stairs two at a time. "What are you still doing inside? Even laborers get a break." She smiled and let him guide her out on the porch and into a redwood chair. San Francisco Bay spread before them like a breathtaking landscape by a famous artist. Sabrina wished they were out on the *Time Lapse,* feeling the wind in their faces and the sea spray on their clothes.

"Lemonade?" Reese asked.

"In a minute," she said, reaching up to catch his hand.

He glanced down at her questioningly but rubbed his thumb over her knuckles.

"You have a really nice house."

"Thank you. It will be nicer once you've settled in. You have some interesting things."

"Mostly junk," she said.

"No, you have some real treasures."

"Nothing I own costs more than fifty dollars."

"But you have memories behind those pieces. Like the doilies your grandmother crocheted for you and the ceramic coffee mugs your mother made. None of my stuff has a story."

She wanted to tell him they'd buy things together and create a story for them. The story of Reese and Sabrina. But in her heart she was a little afraid of that story. Reese made her feel more than she'd ever felt before. She was pregnant and riding high on both joy and anxiety.

He hugged her close to his body and they sat in silence for a few minutes. His words about her belongings touched her. And though she knew that Reese preferred for her to believe he was cold on the inside, she knew that he wasn't. He'd unwittingly given her a glimpse of the longings in his soul. And she wanted to fill them all for him.

"Ready for that lemonade?"

"Yes, please."

He left quietly and Sabrina sat in silence, letting her new house and situation settle around her. Had she made the right choice? She loved Reese for better or worse and she had to be with him. If only she could convince him that she was worthy of his love.

Eight

Three weeks later, Reese still felt raw. Never in his life had he been surrounded by so much comfort. It made him edgy and restless. He hated the softness that Sabrina was bringing to his rough-lonely life, yet at the same time he craved it more than he did his next breath.

Reese walked in from work to find dinner on the table, the newspaper next to his recliner and a set of casual clothes on the bed. The smells of garlic and oregano filled the air and a soft feminine voice sang off-key.

Walls he'd hope to keep in place trembled. No one had ever cared enough for him to take the time to prepare his dinner. The old scars on his back itched. He almost felt the old man hitting him with a belt. Telling him he was too lazy to ever have anything of value in his life.

Reese had succeeded despite his upbringing, and despite his father's death when Reese was sixteen. He'd scrimped and saved and invested with shrewd care to prove the old man wrong. And he had, by God. But this thing with Sabrina… Part of him believed the old man was right. Maybe he didn't deserve a woman like her.

Though a lot of the little things she did for him were nice and kind of outdated, he liked them. At heart, he supposed he was an old-fashioned man. He hated change. This change was hard to take. Harder than he'd thought it would be when he'd pushed for marriage.

The same protective, possessive instincts that had screamed for him to make Sabrina his and bring her under his roof now urged him to push her away. But every night he turned to her. Needing her soft female body to soothe the savageness of his soul. Needing her humid warmth to sheath his flesh and bring him to the only home he'd ever felt on this earth. Needing Sabrina more than he ever wanted to.

Part of his problem was that Sabrina seemed so obvious in her affection for him that he was dying inside. He felt out of control for the first time in years—really out of control in a way that worried him. He didn't trust his emotions or the spark of longing he felt.

The past had taught him that safety lay in not wanting things. His father had once taken all of his toys and burned them just to prove that Reese owned nothing. Over time he'd come to accept that life offered Reese Howard little in the way of comfort.

He dumped his briefcase in the den and went to find his wife. It was time to enforce some of the boundaries they'd agreed to in this marriage. He hated playing the heavy, but a glance at his own reflection in the hall mirror confirmed it was a role he was destined to play.

He was a tough man who'd led an even harder life. Fate should have watched out more closely for Sabrina MacFadden Howard. Fate should have guarded her sweet treasure instead of sending her to him. Fate should have guided her to a better man. A softer man, a man more suited to be her mate instead of the dark loner who craved her the way all creatures of night craved the full light of day.

"Sabrina?" he called.

"In here," she said. He found her in the kitchen singing along with a Dave Matthews CD. Her hips swayed to the beat as she chopped carrots. He froze in the doorway.

A deep feeling of despair swamped him. This was the very thing he'd always wanted. The very woman he'd always craved. And he couldn't indulge himself. He had to step back.

Step back, he ordered himself, and found that he couldn't. It was like being offered a taste of heaven and knowing he was consigned to hell. He wanted to take what was offered and damn the consequences. But he knew the piper always had to be paid and Sabrina didn't deserve to pay for a situation that wasn't her making.

"I hope you're hungry," she said, pivoting to face him. Her heart-shaped face shone with joy, and though she looked a little tired, she seemed to glow from within.

She had the slightest hint of a belly and he knew she'd taken to wearing her pants unbuttoned for comfort. Tonight she wore one of his old shirts and a pair of leggings. Damn, there was nothing wrong with her legs. Long and endless. He wanted to turn off the stove and make love to her on the kitchen table.

He was so hungry he was afraid he'd gorge himself and leave nothing in his wake, like the evil Dracula whose very nature demanded he prey on the one woman he'd love for all time.

Regretting what he had to do but knowing that there was no alternative, he stepped into the kitchen. He ran a hand through his hair, searching for words that were hard to say. "I ate on my way home from work. I'm meeting the guys for a volleyball game."

"Oh," she said, turning back to the sink. Sabrina's pale face reflected clearly in the small window that overlooked the dark backyard. He couldn't be sure but he thought she bit her lip.

Damn, she sounded lost. She sounded small and alone. He'd bet his boat she was crying. Oh, God, she sounded like he felt deep inside. Like he'd felt years before. This was why he'd never stayed with a woman for any length of time. He always hurt them. And then they always abandoned him.

When her shoulders trembled, he wanted to go to her and hug her. To pull her against his big chest and tell her he'd keep her hurts away. But he knew that wasn't a good answer.

"I forgot to call," he said. As an apology it stunk and it did little to make him feel better. He should just keep his mouth shut. He should tell her the truth and stay here in the home she'd created out of his empty house and eat dinner with her.

But for some reason he dug himself deeper instead. "We're practicing for the Cal King Tournament that's going to be in Santa Cruz in July."

"No problem. It's just lasagna and we can heat it up for dinner another night."

She sounded calmer. Damn, he wished she'd turn and face him. He wanted to see her beautiful blue eyes and figure out her thoughts.

"Great," he said, though he felt anything but. Only the sure knowledge that any encouragement now would cause her ten times as much pain later kept him walking out of the kitchen. He heard her follow him down the long tiled hallway and found that he didn't have the courage to face her.

He didn't really want to see her eyes for fear that they'd reflect the hurt and sadness he'd heard in her voice. He sensed her watching him leave. And knew he was a fool to be going out into the cold evening alone when he had everything any sane man would desire waiting right here. But at the moment he wasn't feeling rational. That more than anything else spurred him forward.

"I'll see you later," he called over his shoulder

but didn't look back. There were some things a man should never see and his woman's tears were one of them.

Silence greeted Sabrina when she let herself into the house. It wasn't that late, only 10:00 p.m. If she hadn't seen Reese's car in the garage she would've thought the house was empty. She knew he was here and dreaded seeing him. He hadn't seemed angry on the phone when he'd called to tell her he'd be home early and was looking forward to whatever dinner she had planned.

The anger she'd been ignoring for the last few weeks sprang to life, and she'd informed Reese that she'd made plans for the evening and wouldn't be home. Though there was nothing more that Sabrina wanted to do than spend time at home with Reese, she knew she couldn't be a doormat in her own marriage. He was a strong man, but if she let him ride roughshod over her once, he'd continue to do so. She knew his actions were not out of any sort of need to dominate her, but to prevent her from caring for him. He was too late.

So she'd spent four hours watching a double feature of two of the lousiest movies Hollywood had ever produced. Then took the long way home. She didn't want to see Reese all sweaty and male from his volleyball practice. So close yet so far away.

At first she'd thought her own fear of telling him about the scar from her distant past, her miscarriage, had created the distance. But soon she had realized Reese kept her at bay. She didn't know how to bridge the gap because, as much as she cared for him, she wanted to protect a part of herself.

Now, as she stood in the cold, dark foyer, apprehension settled over her. Regret wasn't far behind. She hated behaving childishly, but there was only so much she could take before she snapped and reacted from the gut instead of with the responses she'd cultivated in her years as a mature adult.

She set her purse and keys on the hall table. The jingling sound echoed in the quiet. She wondered if Reese was sleeping. It was kind of early for him, but that would be a relief. She'd even sleep on the couch so as not to disturb him.

Kicking her shoes off under the deacon's bench, she wrinkled her nose. A different scent floated on the air. The distant call of a foghorn on San Francisco Bay sounded. Was a window open?

She identified the scent as a cigar. The acrid smell led her through the deserted house to the porch. Someone was on the porch. Sabrina's body recognized Reese before her eyes did. Her pulse picked up as she took in the skintight jeans and relaxed pose.

Reese was silhouetted in the moonlight. It painted him in shadows, and Sabrina realized that this was the one place Reese was most comfortable. If he had his way he'd spend his life in half-light.

Sabrina shivered again in her sweater. With his bare chest and feet, Reese seemed immune to the cold breeze. For a minute she wondered if he were human. He often acted like an android devoid of human feeling, but his scars had made her believe that he had good reason to hide. She was tired of him hiding from her.

A bottle hung loosely from Reese's right hand, dangling toward the floor. The smoking cigar was clasped in his left. Sabrina crossed the threshold and stood by his chair. She felt as if she was sixteen again. Actually, being sixteen would have been a blessing because she would have had the hope of youth. Life had taught her some tough lessons, and it appeared that school was not yet out.

"Reese?"

The illuminated boats dotting San Francisco Bay complimented the night stars to make a pretty picture. Out of nowhere Sabrina remembered the phrase—"pretty is as pretty does." Her facade of a marriage came to mind.

Suddenly anger exploded through her body. All the nights when she'd sat home alone at a table set for two came back to her. He'd pushed for this marriage and he'd treated her like his jailer. Actually, he'd treated her like something lower.

"Have fun tonight?" he asked.

The sarcasm in his voice made her flinch. She reminded herself that he'd set and enforced the boundaries of their marriage.

No, she thought. I wish we'd been together like we were on the boat before I was pregnant. But that man had disappeared before the wedding.

"Yes, I did," she answered finally.

"Whom did you go out with?" he asked.

She shrugged and moved farther onto the porch.

Reese's eyes glowed in the dark. She wondered if he realized how intimidating he could be.

"Just some friends."

"What friends?" he asked, swinging his feet to the side of the reclining lounge chair. He put the cigar between his teeth and puffed once.

Settling gingerly on the seat next to him, she said, "From work."

"Can you be more specific?" he asked. He set the bottle down with more force than was necessary.

"Can you?" she demanded. If he wanted a fight she was more than willing.

Reese pinned her with an icy glare. "What does that mean?"

"What do you think it means? You're the one who's playing volleyball with the guys every night. Who are they?"

Sabrina trusted that Reese had told her the truth, though she'd had friends do the same only to find out later that their husbands had been fooling around. Reese had a core of integrity that she'd never encountered in anyone else. Not every man would have pushed for a wedding after a one-night stand.

"If it bothered you, I wish you would have told me."

Sabrina looked up from her clenched hands, leaning forward. She knew she had his attention, and she responded with the honesty that she wanted to mark her marriage from this point on. She wasn't spending four hours wasting time at a movie theater again. "No, you don't."

Reese leaned in also. Reaching across the small space, he ran a rough finger down the side of her cheek. Tears threatened to fall at the tender look in his eyes. God, he could be so tender sometimes. He was such a complex man—would she ever really know him?

"You're right. I like my space. But that doesn't mean I like you doing the same thing."

Silence descended but there was no comfort in it. Sabrina's emotions ricocheted in her head. Her heart screamed at her to just pull Reese close and smother him in her love. Her head wanted her to protect herself. And her body yearned for the sweet comfort only to be found in his arms.

"Reese, you were the one who said we'd live separate lives."

He gave her one of the saddest smiles she'd ever seen. Her soul longed to reach out to that melancholy man. But she stayed where she was.

"I did, didn't I?" There was a wistful note in his voice.

"Yes." Tears burned her eyes again, and this time she thought they might fall because her emotion grew as she saw in his eyes a glimpse of the affection he held for her.

"Well I changed my mind," he said quietly.

"Why?" she asked.

"Maybe because I've been sitting here alone since six and I don't think I could do this again. Maybe because I understand what I've been doing to you night after night and it's not working. Maybe because…ah, hell, Sabrina, I care for you."

Her heart lifted a little bit. "Really?"

"Really."

He reached across the space between their chairs and drew her over the small distance, cradling her between his legs. His head rested on her midriff, and his warm breath trickled through the layer of her shirt.

Her nipples tightened. She threaded her fingers in his thick hair and held him closer to her. She wanted to offer him the solace of her body. She wanted him in a way those hurried, middle-of-the-night love-makings hadn't fulfilled. She wanted to show Reese she understood what he'd been trying to say.

She longed to comfort this man who, in his own words, had been raised like a mangy dog left to wander the streets. She wanted to shower the love she felt all over him. He was so much more than just the perfect lover of her dreams. Deep inside, Sabrina wondered if she had the depth to really love him as he needed to be loved.

Reese reached for the buttons on her blouse. "God, woman, you don't know what you do to me."

Sabrina wondered if it was a tenth of what he did to her.

The summer sun burned into his back as Reese stood in the sand waiting for the ball. Beach volleyball was a sport he enjoyed with a passion. He and Jeff were competing in the Cal King Tournament. He scanned the crowd gathered behind the ropes and found Sabrina standing next to Mimi, Jeff's wife.

Their two children, towheaded boys who resembled their dad, stood next to Sabrina.

His wife. Lately, he'd wanted her with him everywhere he went. She smiled at him, and he had the insane desire to pose for her. To flex the muscles he'd honed through years of living life to the fullest. Unlike the other guys who played bare-chested, Reese wore a tank top. In fact, Sabrina was probably the only person alive who knew about the scars.

His previous lovers hadn't been as perceptive as she was, which suited him. But he found that he wanted more with Sabrina than he had had with other women. *He had since the beginning.*

"Stop making eyes at your wife and pay attention," Jeff yelled.

Reese looked up in time to save the ball from going out of bounds and set Jeff up perfectly for a spike, which Jeff executed. Then, grinning widely, he shoved his hands into the air and shook his butt. The winning point.

Reese envied Jeff the security he had in himself. There was a comic element to his best friend that Reese knew he'd never have. Life had been hard for him. So hard that he'd never consider doing a silly dance when he scored a winning point.

Reese and Jeff exchanged high fives and shook hands with the other team. Sabrina hurried onto the court, bringing PowerAde, a towel and Mike, Jeff's oldest son. He was struck by what a strange and rare gift he'd been given.

"Good game," she said.

"Yeah, Mr. Howard. Great going. I really loved that spike you made."

Reese smiled down at Mike. He'd never really interacted with kids and was a little distant usually, but Sabrina loved kids. She was always baby-sitting for her friends or inviting Jeff's family over for the day. She was forcing him out of his shell and he wasn't sure he liked it.

"Thanks."

"I didn't realize how intense the game was," Sabrina said.

He watched her closely, certain she was getting at some point but not clear on what it was.

"I'm sorry I made such a big deal about sitting at home alone for a few nights," she said at last.

Mike's attention was diverted by a hermit crab and the boy wandered a few feet away from them.

For once, Reese allowed his reflexes to take control. He pulled Sabrina against his chest and savored the feel of *his* woman in *his* arms. "I was using the practice as an excuse to keep distance between us."

"You were?"

"Yes. All the other guys brought girlfriends or wives to the practice sessions. I—"

He leaned backward and stared down at her, trying to find the words he didn't know how to express. He was used to keeping people at bay. Everyone, even the guys he hung out with after work. He didn't know how to tear down barriers and wanted to at least find a way to let Sabrina closer. *But not all the way past his walls.*

"Can I watch you practice in the future?" she

asked, saving him from having to form words that would clearly show his vulnerability.

"Yes, I'm past denying that you have an effect on me."

Shyly she glanced up at him from under her lashes. She was so sexy without even trying; it got to him every time. "Do I affect you?"

"You know you do," he said, brushing his mouth against her hair. She smelled so fresh, and he was so sweaty and hot. She was always his opposite. Always cleaner than he was.

"Good," she said, nipping his lip.

"Where's Mike?" she asked, as if suddenly realizing the child was gone.

"Over there," Reese said. There was an incipient panic in Sabrina's voice that he didn't understand.

"Mike, come back over here," she called. Her belly protruded against the front of her shirt and she reached for Mike's hand as if she were afraid something would happen to the boy. She was protective of the kid. He realized that she was always careful of herself and small children. When they'd baby-sat Kayla and Larry's kids last weekend she'd been the same way.

Sabrina was the kind of woman who should've married a man with a normal upbringing. Instead she was smiling at him, sweeping her gaze down his sweaty body and watching him through half-lowered eyelids. She had that look on her face that she always wore when they made love.

He felt his body harden in a rush and wondered how long he'd have to stay before they could leave.

He needed to make love to his wife. He'd been using sex to bind her to him. He'd come too close to losing her a few weeks ago. He wasn't sure what was needed to make her stay, but the more ties he could find to hold her—without having to all-out love her—the happier he'd be.

Jeff, Mimi and Kyle joined them. The flower scent of Sabrina's perfume swept around him and brought memories of the early morning when they'd been getting dressed on the boat. They'd sailed down to Santa Cruz last night, and it had been close quarters getting ready this morning.

"Let's go celebrate," Jeff suggested.

"Let's hit one of the open bars down the beach," Mimi said.

Jeff and Mimi gathered their brood and started down the beach. Reese knew they should be moving along, but instead he cuddled Sabrina closer to him. He wanted to celebrate with her and her alone. Reese's shorts grew snug as he remembered Sabrina brushing past him in the companionway. God, he wished he'd had time to make love to her then. He remembered her sweet, curvy, bare body and wanted her that way again.

Reese wrapped his arm around her and directed her off the playing court. He knew he'd been given a gift and decided it was time to show Sabrina how much it meant to him that she would have his child. How much it meant to him that she wanted him home every night. How much it meant to him that she cared.

Nine

Reese moved around the kitchen like a man sure of his domain. Tantalizing aromas filled the air, and after the day she'd had, Sabrina was glad to put her feet up and let him wait on her.

"What are you fixing for dinner?" she asked, sipping the sparkling water Reese had given her when she came in from work.

"Pan-fried trout, salad and stir-fried veggies." He wore her Kiss the Cook apron and should have looked silly but didn't.

"Wow, is it a prepackaged meal?" she asked.

"Hell, no." He looked offended, which made her smile.

"You can cook?" she asked. This was a side to Reese she'd never seen before.

"Of course I can cook. I've lived alone for the last fifteen years. It was either this or eat out every night, and I can't stand crowds."

"Me, neither," she said quietly.

"I know." She smiled at him this time. Just one of the million little things they had in common.

"Well, now that I know you can cook, you can have that job."

"Why?"

"Because I hate it. I'm not good at it, either."

"You do just fine," he said.

The phone rang before she could comment on the fact that he was always defending her, even against herself. Reese answered the phone and Sabrina sat back and watched him. She let the sound of his voice brush over her senses.

"Sabrina?"

"Yes?"

"Phone," he said, and passed it to her.

It was Kayla asking her to watch her kids for the night. Larry was on a business trip and Kayla's sister-in-law had gone into labor.

"Sure, bring them over."

"Thanks, pal. I owe you one. I'll baby-sit your baby one night so you and Reese can go out."

"No problem."

Sabrina hung up the phone and briefly touched her belly. She couldn't wait to hold her child. Sometimes her arms felt empty and she wanted desperately to have the baby. Other times she remembered her first pregnancy and worried that she'd do something to endanger the baby.

"Kayla needs me to baby-sit her kids. Do you mind if they spend the night?"

"I don't mind," he said quietly.

"I know you like to watch *Sports Center*. I'll keep them out of your way."

He slid the trout out of the pan and onto a plate. "Sabrina, I like Dee and Rosie. Besides, I could use the practice."

"Why?"

"I know nothing about being a dad."

She thought about the only example Reese had had. It wasn't a good one. Did he have doubts, she wondered? He seemed so self-assured.

He moved past her to set her plate in front of her. She grabbed his wrist when he would have moved away. He looked down at her. "I think you're going to be a great father."

He didn't say anything. There seemed to be a spark of hope in his eyes, but he showed no outward reaction. Bending, he brushed a soft kiss against her forehead.

"Thanks."

The phone rang just after they'd all settled onto the sofa to watch the Disney Channel. Kayla's daughters were six and eight and full of questions. Reese excused himself to answer the phone, and Sabrina wondered if he was hoping business would call him away.

"It's for you," he said, bringing the handheld unit with him.

It was her boss, and Sabrina spent twenty minutes

going over the presentation she'd put together for
Raul. Apparently, he'd made a favorable impression
on his superiors that afternoon and they wanted him
to give the presentation to the parent company the
next day.

Sabrina shook her head as she walked back into
the living room. No matter how simple they made
technology, the business world would always need
secretaries.

She paused in the doorway. Dee and Rosie were
asleep on Reese. He was sprawled comfortably in
the middle of the sofa and the girls were resting on
either side of him. His strong arms held them pro-
tectively, and Sabrina felt her heart melt. Here was
the man she wanted to see more of. The one who
could love but was afraid to show it.

There was an aching vulnerability on his face as
she watched. She wondered if he were imagining
their child. A child with his dark eyes and her red-
dish hair curled next to him. Maybe a girl?

Oh, God, she couldn't wait to have her baby.
Their child would be a dream come true for her and
maybe the salvation Reese hadn't realized he
needed.

She cleared her throat before entering the room.
Reese glanced over his shoulder. ''I don't know how
this happened.''

The big tough guy sure of himself on any dangerous mountain slope or city street brought to his
knees by two tiny girls. She wished she had a cam-
era.

She bit her tongue to keep from making a light

comment. This was an important moment for Reese
and she hoped he'd realize it.

"I'll take them upstairs," she said.

After the girls were tucked in bed, Sabrina joined
Reese on the sofa to watch a sports cable channel.
She wanted to find out what he felt about the girls,
what he'd been thinking earlier while they slept
against him, but she was afraid to ask.

"Why aren't you a professional athlete?" she
asked instead.

"I never played sports as a youth," he said.

"Why not? It's obvious you love them."

"I wasn't a healthy kid."

"Asthma? Kayla has asthma."

"No, not asthma."

"What, then? It's not anything genetic, is it?"

He maneuvered her so that she was sitting on his
lap facing away from him. His breath was ragged in
her ears and his touch on her shoulders was softer
than dawn breaking through the night.

He found a tight spot in her neck and rubbed
harder to loosen the knot. Sabrina knew she should
try to be clinical about the massage but wasn't coming anywhere close. His touch was like sunlight on
her skin, warm and natural, and created a craving in
her for more.

It occurred to her that he might be trying to avoid
the subject she'd introduced. "What about youth
sports? You're built for football."

She moaned softly as his fingers brushed the sensitive spot at the base of her neck. Sensation spread
downward in waves, tightening her breasts and pool-

ing at her center. Rolling her shoulders, she angled herself under his touch so that he'd massage her there again.

"I didn't want to play sports because I always had unexplainable bruises and broken bones."

She felt tears sting her eyes. Oh, God. No one should have to endure what he'd endured. "Oh, Reese."

She tried to turn in his embrace, needing to kiss him and caress his dear face. To reassure both of them that he was healthy and whole now. But he wouldn't let her move.

He hugged her tight, and she closed her eyes as he rested his forehead on her shoulder. "Oh, Sabrina."

She didn't know what to say or how to right this wrong. And sometimes talking only made things worse and more real. After a few moments he loosened his hold on her and resumed his steady kneading of her tight shoulders.

"What did you do today?" he asked. His deep voice played over her senses like rain over the hot desert sand.

Never had Sabrina shared the intimate details of her life with anyone. But tonight she wanted to finish the small talk and take her husband to bed. To caress his scarred body and heal him. She wondered what he'd do if she turned around, took off her clothes and seduced him while the television played quietly in the background.

"A last-minute presentation. Raul has a problem

with deadlines.'' She loved her boss, but every once in a while he pushed her past her limits.

Reese laughed. ''I take it he won't anymore?''

''No, he'll still have the problem. Next time he won't stand over my shoulder while I prepare his presentation. I'm afraid I lost my temper.'' Sabrina was still amazed at the emotions that had charged through her when her boss had walked into her office at four-thirty and informed her he needed a forty-slide presentation for a five o'clock meeting.

''I didn't know you had a temper,'' Reese said carefully.

''I don't. I think it must be a pregnancy thing.''

''Poor Raul.''

''Raul was just fine.''

''I'm not,'' Reese said, directly into her ear.

''Why not?'' she asked, leaning back on his chest and looking up at him.

''Because I'm not kissing you.''

Reese bent and took her mouth. There was none of the practiced seduction he'd used the first time they'd made love. Not that she'd have suspected they were practiced moves, only being with him later had shown her the difference.

His lips were firm and hard. Moving over her own mouth with the sureness of a surgeon on a critical care patient. The sweetness of the fruit juice he'd been drinking and the unique Reese taste enticed Sabrina to delve farther into his mouth. She reached up behind her head and buried her fingers in his hair.

Reese broke the kiss with several little nibbles of her lips. ''Enough for now.''

Yeah, right. She felt the proof of desire stirring against her backside. "I'm not really watching this sports show."

"I'm not, either."

"Then let's go to bed," Sabrina said.

"No. I'm trying to be more than your lover."

You are, she thought. But Reese wasn't ready to hear that. And honestly, Sabrina admitted, she wasn't ready to say it.

"Besides, the girls are sleeping in the room next to ours upstairs."

Silence fell. Sabrina leaned back against Reese's legs and let his body heat seep through her clothing. She loved the heady feeling of being surrounded by him. Of being protected by him. Of being loved by him?

She'd been showering him with her affection but held a part of herself back. Though she knew Reese needed only to be shown love *to* love, she didn't want to make herself completely vulnerable to him. Once she did that, she'd have everything to lose if he didn't return her emotions.

"How was your day?" she asked to distract herself from her thoughts.

"Talked to that woman from the clinic."

"What woman?"

"The inseminated one."

The bitterness in his tone surprised her. "You don't like her?"

"I don't care about her either way."

She moved around to face him. He'd lost all the laughter and sensuality he'd had a few minutes ago.

"Why not?"

"I don't think women should have children by themselves."

"I was going to."

"I know," he said quietly.

"Did you feel this way about me, too?"

"Yes."

"Do you now?"

"We're married. You're not having a child by yourself."

"But if I'd decided not to marry you?"

"Sabrina, it's a moot point."

Sabrina stood, shaking with anger for the second time that day. No wonder Reese wasn't making any declarations of undying devotion.

"How do you feel about me?"

"I don't know."

Reese surged to his feet. Pulling her into his body, he hugged her so tightly that her anger evaporated as quickly as it had been born. He was holding her as if he'd never let her go.

"I don't know," he repeated, his hands stroking down her back. "But I don't want to fight with you."

And for now that was enough for Sabrina.

A small baby lay in the middle of the deck of the *Time Lapse*—crying. A storm raged in the distance. As Reese tried to cross the slippery deck he felt the biting sting of his father's belt across his back. He clenched his body and ignored the pain as he had in the past. He had to get to the baby. Where was Sabrina?

He glanced frantically around the deck of the boat and found his wife, unconscious on the deck. He had to help her. A child's cry ripped through the night.

Had to save the baby—

"Reese?"

The soft voice called him from the storm but he was reluctant to leave. He had to protect the child, and save his wife. A crucial urgency drove him toward the child and Sabrina. Before he could reach the baby, a huge wave swept over the side of the boat and the baby and Sabrina disappeared under the seething water.

"Reese, wake up."

He felt a light touch on his shoulder and rolled from it. He needed to save the baby, save his wife.

"Reese, dammit—"

Fighting to leave the depths of sleep behind, he sat up and swung his legs over the side of the bed. He buried his head in his hands and waited for the nightmare to recede. Slowly he felt his heartbeat begin to slow, but that image remained.

Sabrina's hand on his back soothed the emotions roiling inside of him but he flinched away from her, not wanting to be comforted. His mind still felt the sting of his father's blows and the picture of the child swept under the waves.

"You okay?" Sabrina asked, her silky, sleep-saturated voice brushing over senses that were not quite normal. His tentative hold on his emotions grew more tenuous.

"Yeah," he said, not facing her. Would the past never leave him alone? Was he doomed to repeat the mistakes of his father? Was his dream a warning as Sabrina's time drew nearer? He'd never wanted to be a father but, by his own insistence, he was now going to be active in the upbringing of his own child.

What the hell had he been thinking?

He had to back away and fast. The bed dipped as Sabrina rolled closer to him and embraced his waist. Her fragile arms held him tightly. He hoped she didn't sense the weakness and doubt within him. He wanted to accept the comfort of her sweet body but knew his dream was a message. One he couldn't ignore.

She brushed her lips against his back, then sought out the faded scars. He gritted his teeth against the need to sweep her into his arms. He couldn't.

Not now.

Unchecked violence flowed through his veins, as did the need for retribution that had been denied him when he'd been a young man. Now, the dream fresh in his mind, memories alive in his head, he needed to release his pent-up rage.

His cry of outrage strangled him. Choking him as it stayed against the back of his throat. Why were the assumptions of other men out of reach for him?

Or were those assumptions of a happy family— wife and kids—not really achievable for most men? Why could he overcome only physical challenges?

He carefully removed her arms from his body and stood. The moonlight spilled through the window he'd left open and painted shadows across Sabrina's body. She was curled on her side, her belly a small swell against a flannel nightshirt, and her hair a dark, luxurious mass on the light linens.

He'd been trying to bridge the gap between them that he'd created when he'd excluded her from his life. But the bridge wasn't a sturdy one. His efforts were halfhearted, and he knew Sabrina sensed it. Seeing her pregnant body brought everything into focus. Now he knew why. He wasn't only afraid of being like his dad and harming the baby, he was afraid of losing her the way he'd lost his mom.

"Where are you going?" she asked, sitting up and serious, the lassitude left by sleep now gone from her eyes. She had a grave look, and he felt meaner than a predator striking its unsuspecting prey.

"Out."

"Will you be back?"

He shrugged. He wasn't committing himself to anything else until he found a way to make this relationship work for him. Sabrina engendered in him emotions he wasn't prepared to handle.

He tugged his jeans up over his legs. She watched him with her big blue eyes. Eyes that had at first sparked a deep-seated recognition within him. Eyes that had called to his soul and promised relaxation and solace. But now they promised... He didn't know what they promised. And he had no idea how he would come to a decision that would work for him and her.

He walked to the closet and pulled on a black button-down shirt. He slid his feet into his shoes while standing. He didn't want to sit on the edge of the bed.

Well, that was wrong. He wanted to be close to her. To feel her breath against his flesh, her warmth along his cold, cold body and her heart beating solidly against his chest. But he knew now that he couldn't, so instead he stood and pretended he couldn't see her. His hands trembled as he dropped to his haunches and tied his shoelaces.

He slid his wallet into his pocket and grabbed his keys.

"Reese?"

Her body was painted in the light of the moon-shadowed bed. Even at a distance he could see that her eyes glittered and he knew that once again he'd brought tears to the one woman he never wanted to see cry.

He started for the door, needing to escape from the emotional ties threatening to consume him.

"Be careful," Sabrina said softly.

Reese walked away cursing himself and the bastard who'd raised him.

Sabrina hadn't expected an apology from Reese for the way he'd left her the previous evening. In fact, she'd been surprised when he'd called her at work to make sure she'd made it into the office okay. The fog had been heavy and he knew she hated driving in it. Her throat had closed, and she'd barely been able to whisper that she was fine.

She hadn't expected him to send red roses and plead for forgiveness, but she'd hoped for it. Hoped for some sign that Reese might realize the impact his actions had had on her. When he'd called her earlier in the day it had been easy to keep the hope burning. But when he walked through the front door for dinner, she knew her hopes were in vain—the tender lover she wanted to see was hidden deep within the battle-hardened warrior.

Sabrina didn't know what to do when Reese returned later the next evening. *She loved the man.* Loved his excitement and passion for the outdoors and for beach volleyball. Loved that he knew all the answers to the morning crossword puzzles but would never gloat about it. Loved that he'd gone through a lot of trouble to make her feel like his house was now her home.

He meant more to her than any other person alive today, but something had to give. The very real fear that she'd break first had kept her from paging him in the middle of the night and begging him to come back. For all that he'd given her, Reese had not given her the one thing she craved.

His love.

She'd settle for genuine deep caring if he'd show it consistently. But he never did. And she was beginning to believe he never would. Staying with him, marrying him, had been the worst mistake she'd ever made.

Reese stood silhouetted in the doorway between

the dark hallway and the kitchen. The outside light trickled in through the panel glass by the front door, casting his face half in shadows. It should have made him look sinister or menacing.

Instead, he looked tired. His dark eyes were heavy with suppressed emotion and he held his body stiffly as if he expected a wounding blow. She wanted to wrap her arms around him and cradle him at her breasts, to offer him the comfort of her body. But she could tell by the bleak expression on his face that he wouldn't accept solace from her.

The thought so staggered her, she stepped away from Reese, who stood stock-still in the doorway, watching her. His jeans and black shirt looked nice, she thought inanely. He appeared to be a normal, average, happy man. Only Sabrina knew the truth. He was far from that illusion and he always would be.

The baby kicked, startling Sabrina. The baby had been moving for a while now, but the sudden position changes in her womb never failed to surprise her. She'd created another being…with Reese. Sabrina smiled to herself as she cradled her stomach.

"Did the baby move?" Reese asked, awe filling his face as he took a small step forward. His gaze fixed on her belly where the small limb pushed against it. The thermal top she was wearing was only a thin layer of cloth, and the outline of a small foot could be seen.

Reese started forward, his hand extended, but stopped before he reached her. A look of extreme pain crossed his face. Everything became clear in an instant.

She'd been kidding herself.

Reese wasn't going to wake up one morning and be a cheerful-go-lucky guy, happy to have found himself in a situation that he'd carefully avoided his entire life. There was not going to be a sudden epiphany where he smacked himself on the head and said, *Wow! Look what I've had all this time.*

Whatever emotion Reese felt for her, it wasn't love. There wasn't a deep well of caring waiting just outside her reach. Only the living pain of memories and the harsh reality of duty had brought her and Reese together. That was the glue that bound their marriage.

There was no love to be found in Reese Howard. She'd been pouring all of her emotion down a drain. Showering on him the one thing he would never accept from her. The one thing he *couldn't* accept.

The stresses of a long day at work, a sore back from the pregnancy and the fact that reality had chosen today to hit her over the head nearly undid her. A bone-deep weariness spread throughout her body. She wished she could cry but realized she'd cried her last tears on Reese. She'd spent last night lying alone in his big bed where he'd repeatedly brought her body to the heights of pleasure.

The baby kicked again. She wondered if the small being had somehow picked up on her agitation. She was sure it had. Hadn't she read in one of the books about their remarkable perception?

"Are you okay?" Reese asked. His genuine concern added another layer to the pain she felt at not knowing his true affection.

Afraid to speak, she nodded. She felt as if she were either going to melt into a mass of hurt or turn into an angry fishwife. Sabrina acknowledged wryly that good money lay on the fishwife.

He dropped his attaché case and coat on one of the kitchen chairs and ran his hands through his hair. It was longish again and fell rakishly over his forehead.

"I'm…"

Sorry. She knew that was what he was trying to say. But she didn't believe him anymore.

Finding her voice and backbone, Sabrina braced her hands on the back of one of the chairs, using it to support her through what she had to do.

"We can't go on like this," she began.

"I know."

"I think I should move out."

"No."

The word was soft but emphatic.

"Reese, be reasonable. I'm torturing you."

"You're not. I'm trying, Sabrina. I really am."

"I know, and that's the worst part. Seeing you tear yourself up over something you can't control. I just can't do it anymore."

She realized she could still cry as she felt the warm, wet tracks on her face. "I love you. But I can't live with you anymore."

"Sabrina—"

"No, don't say anything yet," she said, crossing the room and brushing his hard mouth with her fingers. "This isn't at all what I'd anticipated when I decided to be inseminated. I was going to have the procedure for selfish reasons, because I was lonely. I'm doing this for you and the baby."

"I don't want you to leave."

Sabrina waited, wanting to hear the words she knew she wouldn't. "You don't want me to stay, either."

Sabrina brushed past him, picked up her purse and keys from the hall table and walked out the door. The chilly night air wrapped around her and the baby kicked again in her womb, but the wonder and joy of the world couldn't touch the layer of pain that had wrapped itself around her soul. Not even when she lay in a cold, lonely hospital bed after losing her first child had she felt so alone.

Ten

I love you. The words echoed in his head like the magical music of a carousel in childhood. No one had ever muttered those words to him, and he felt almost as if they weren't real. Except they were and so was she. She was walking away, leaving him, and she had no intention of coming back. He had to make her stay here with him. Without her he had nothing. He'd be back to where he'd been before she entered his life—quietly filling empty spaces he hadn't realized existed.

He had no real concept of what his feelings for her were, but he knew with gut-deep certainty that if he let her leave it would be the biggest mistake of his life.

He sprinted the short distance down the hall and

out onto the landing where the lights of the bay and the city were barely visible through the low layering of fog.

"Sabrina, wait."

Reese cursed himself for a bastard as he chased after his crying wife. Boy, it really made a man feel like pond scum to reduce a woman to tears. A pregnant woman, no less. A woman who *loved* him.

He reached out and grabbed her shoulder, careful to keep his touch light. He didn't want to be one of those men who lost sight of their strength when they were angry. He'd always prided himself on his control, but since he'd met Sabrina control was a distant memory.

"Please, Reese."

She was stiff. Reese wanted to pull her safely into his arms, hold her against his chest and rest his hands over the child he wanted more than he'd expected to. The child that was slowly changing his focus on life along with the woman who carried it.

Emotion choked him. He turned his face to the wind. The cold, biting wind burned his skin. He saw Sabrina shiver. She wrapped her arms around her body.

Seeing her hold herself away from him brought home how much pain he'd inflicted on her. Inflicted on the one woman who meant the most to him. He didn't understand exactly what it was he felt for her. He had no other experience to compare it to, but knew that if he let her walk away from him now he'd regret it.

He tugged her into his arms, held her tightly.

Reese never wanted to let her go but she was right. Something had to give. He couldn't keep pushing her away and expecting her to stay here with him. Couldn't keep the distance he wanted emotionally and the closeness he craved physically.

He buried his head in the soft hair curling at the back of her neck and breathed deeply. She smelled like a cold fall evening. Her skin was luminous in the moonlight, and her ripe body tempted him to take her to bed and forget about their argument and the very real problems that had brought them here.

"Don't go, honey."

"I'm losing myself, Reese. I'm becoming the woman I was at eighteen and I don't want to be that person again."

"I don't want you to lose yourself," he said. He meant it. He hated to think he was tearing her down while she'd been building him up. While she'd been showing him a totally different way to live. One that didn't involve taking to the sea when times got tough but staying and working through the problems.

The breeze blew and she shivered in his arms. "Let's go inside."

He took her hand but she didn't step forward.

He looked at her. Her expression so serious and sad, he ached.

"Don't make me believe that things will be different and then keep shoving me away, Reese. If I come inside now and leave again—I won't come back." The graveness of her tone convinced him of her sincerity. But Reese knew that after tonight he couldn't ask her to come back to him again.

How many times could he push her away and expect her to come back? How many times could he expect her to forgive him for the past? How many times did he have to pay for the childhood that had shaped him into the man he was today?

He knew he had to convince her to stay. Had to look inside himself and find something that would make her believe she meant something to him. That she was important to him just by being herself. By being the funny woman who couldn't do the crossword puzzle on her own. By wearing his old shirts with a flare that never failed to amaze him. By quietly loving and supporting him.

"It'll be different. I'll be different." The words were meant to convince them both, he realized.

"Why the sudden change of heart?" she asked.

He looked down into her face. Her blue eyes looked black in the dim light. *Heart.* The word haunted him. The one that made him want to give her his all. But would his all be enough?

"Do you really love me?" he asked, his voice husky and low.

She bit her lip and nodded.

His hands trembled and his groin tightened. He needed to cement the fragile bonds she'd extended with her confession. He wanted to wrap her so tightly to him that she'd never again leave him.

But with the physical demand came the knowledge that he walked a fine line. If he pushed too hard and too fast he'd lose her. *Maybe for good.* "I don't understand how."

She caged his face with her cold hands. *Her touch, so gentle.* No one's hands on his flesh had ever been so kind.

"Me, neither. I only know I need you more than I've ever needed anyone in my life."

"Oh, baby," he said, lowering his head and taking her mouth. The soft mouth that had uttered words he hadn't even known he'd needed to hear until she'd said them. The mouth that had been calling him from the darkness of the past for as long as he'd known her.

The mouth that tasted like every erotic dream he'd ever had and every secret dream he'd always searched for. Dreams his volleyball buddies would have scoffed at and his boss would have believed to be untrue. His longing for a nice, safe routine and an ordinary life.

He slid his hands down her back, feeling the fragile length of her spine, the rounded curves of her buttocks. Her feminine flesh waited for him. He needed her now.

She nestled against his chest, her head resting above his heart. The cold organ would never feel anything for another person. Except that for some reason it felt as if Sabrina had taken up residence there.

He lifted her into his arms and carried her back into the house. Using his foot, he kicked the door shut. The silence in the house settled around them. The only sounds were their breathing. Her breath brushed his neck and her fingers tunneled through his hair.

He loved the way she responded to him, as if no other man had ever touched her the way he did. No other man in the world could bring her what he did. And she touched him in a way no other woman had, understanding about the scars on his back and the emotional bonds that had always been missing from his life.

She lifted her face from his shoulder, her lips seeking his in the darkened hallway. Her mouth was perfectly formed and tempted him to linger all day on her lips. To start kissing her and never stop. Not until he was buried hilt-deep inside her tight sheath and she was too weak to moan his name.

"I need you, Sabrina," he said, praying she didn't realize he needed her for more than the pleasure she gave him in bed. He needed her in ways he didn't want to acknowledge.

"I need you, too, Reese."

"I'm here for you, honey."

He settled her carefully in the center of the bed. Lust racked his body, and he wanted to drive her to the heights of ecstasy again and again. The urgency riding him now wouldn't let up. Relishing in the woman beneath the layers of cloth, he swiftly removed her clothing. Her reddish-brown hair was a dark cloud on the pillow, and the pale skin of her body made him feel as if he would spontaneously combust. She looked like a woman in the full joy of womanhood. Her rounded belly, slim thighs, dark nipples.

He wanted this woman. The woman who was his. The woman who'd given him her heart and soul. The woman who was the mother of his child.

''I can't wait tonight,'' he said, ripping his own clothes from his body. He toed off his loafers and was naked in less than fifteen seconds—and that was too long. He lowered himself over her blossoming body. Bending, he took her nipple in his mouth and sucked strongly but carefully, knowing how sensitive her breasts had become.

He smoothed his hands over her rounded belly, felt the child move within it. And then swept his hand lower. Settling his palm over the heart of her womanhood. Her warmth greeted him, spilling over onto his fingers. He tested her readiness with one finger and then two.

Sabrina moaned, her hips rising from the bed. Her hands clutching at the back of his head, then his shoulders. Nails biting.

''Now, Reese.''

He lifted his head from her breast and braced himself on his forearms. He entered her slowly though every instinct in his body clamored for him to drive home. He needed to make sure she understood how much he cherished her.

He thrust in a steady rhythm, waiting for Sabrina. Needing to feel her body tighten around his and pull him home. Her moans grew louder and her nails dug into his shoulders and the clenching of her muscles pulled him over the edge.

When he came back to himself, he tugged her close against his chest and pulled the covers over them. There in the dark with his heart beating slow and steady, and Sabrina's relaxed breathing washing over his chest, he knew he had to do something to make her stay. He had to show her that she meant more to him than any other woman had, but he also had to protect himself, because he'd only just realized the power she held by threatening to walk away.

Reese was showering Sabrina with the kind of devotion she'd never thought possible. And while she enjoyed the attention, deep inside her terrible secret had grown.

A choice made when she was more a girl than a woman. But the fact that she'd hidden it for so long had made it grow into a huge monster she felt would climb from under her bed one night and attack them both.

Now that Reese had finally decided to let himself enjoy their marriage, she couldn't. The closer it came to her time to deliver the baby the more her worries increased.

A late-term miscarriage would be so much harder to take than the earlier-term one she'd had. She followed the doctor's orders religiously and sometimes Reese teased her about it, but there was nothing more important to her than having his baby.

"Close your eyes," Reese ordered.

Sabrina did. It was better if she didn't look at him now when she was swamped with guilt.

"Reese, I have to talk to you." Not another moment could go by. Reese was an understanding guy underneath his gruff exterior. But he might be hurt that she'd waited so long to tell him.

"Not now. I have a surprise." He brushed his lips over her eyelids and she shivered. God, this man did crazy things to her system. She was turning into a sex maniac, she thought, hoping his surprise was an afternoon in his arms.

"Okay, but after the surprise. It's important. Even if the 49ers are playing, we're going to talk."

"No problem. They're not playing this week."

"Good," she said, and reached out. It was eerie having her eyes closed. Reese had stepped out of her reach. She couldn't even feel the heat of his body. She felt vulnerable. Blindly she thrust her arm into the dark space and encountered Reese's arm.

"Are you peeking?" he asked, and slid his hand around hers. Slowly he knitted their fingers together and their palms rested against each other's.

"No, I'm not. It's weird to have my eyes closed."

"The surprise is worth it," he said, leading her through the house. She felt the Spanish tile under her bare feet and wondered if they were going outside.

"Careful. We're going up the stairs."

She stumbled over the first step and was swept up into his arms. "I'm too heavy, Reese. Put me down."

"You'll never be too heavy."

"Don't go all macho on me. If you're injured, Jeff will kill me. You have that grudge match to play in next weekend."

He snorted.

"Did you snort?"

"Men don't snort."

"Well it sure sounded—"

His lips on hers ended her train of thought. He tasted like the coffee they'd had for breakfast and the omelets she'd made. He was like sunshine on a cold winter day. He was the man who'd become the sun in her world. Now, if she could only get rid of the clouds looming on the horizon.

"Here we are," he said, setting her on her feet.

"I hope we're in the bedroom," she said.

He laughed and kissed her again. This time using his entire body to seduce her. Chest rubbing against her breasts, hands massaging her back and buttocks, pulling her closer to him, mouth claiming hers so deeply that she forgot everything. If her eyes had been open, she would have closed them.

He pulled back. "Open your eyes."

She did and froze. He'd brought her to the upstairs den. His office at home had been converted into a nursery. They'd worked together to paint the room a beautiful sea green and hired an artist to stencil sailing ships and fantasy pictures on the wall.

But the furniture had been in boxes last night. Now it was all arranged in the room. The crib was stuffed with plush animals, and two rockers sat facing the window that overlooked the bay.

A mobile of whales and dolphins hung above the baby's bed and the changing table was piled with clothing so small it was hard to imagine they'd fit anyone.

Tears burned the back of her eyes as she looked

around the room and realized that the man who'd created this room was a man who could love.

"Oh, Reese," she said. It was all she could get out before her throat closed and the tears she'd hoped to control began to fall.

He pulled her to his chest and rocked her slowly back and forth. "I know you wanted to do everything yourself, but the doctor did say no more lifting so I thought I'd take care of this for you."

"Thank you," she said. "I love you."

"I know."

It wasn't the response she wanted. Not the one she'd hoped for. Sabrina pulled back, looked into his eyes and saw the same guarded expression he'd worn for the two weeks since they'd had their argument.

He wasn't in love with her, she realized. He never would be. She was never going to hear those three little words she craved.

She stepped back and walked idly around the room, stopping to touch the baby afghan that lay over the railing of the crib. Their baby would never want for anything material the way Reese had as a child, but would he be able to give the baby more? Would he be able to give her more?

"What's the matter, Sabrina?"

"Nothing," she said.

"Are you sure?" he asked, his eyes dark with concern.

"Yes," she said, knowing if she had to tell him what she wanted to hear, he'd say the words but they wouldn't mean anything to him. And Sabrina wasn't the girl she once was. She'd asked for love once and been burned. She wasn't going to ask for it again.

Reese gave up trying to figure out women. A week had passed since he'd redecorated his retreat into a room for the baby. He had wanted to show Sabrina that he wanted her and the baby in his life without having to open himself up to the emotional entanglements he feared. But his plan had backfired.

Hell, he knew she deserved better, and now it seemed she did, too. There were no more declarations of love. No more cuddling on the couch while *Sports Center* played in the background. No more early-evening boat rides where they dropped anchor and made love with the sea and sky around them.

Dammit, he'd never expected her to leave him emotionally. He'd counted on her to keep pouring her love out and letting him bathe in it.

Geez, he was a moron.

Of course, she didn't have an endless supply of love to keep showering on him. She needed to have her well refilled, and only if he loved her would that happen. But he couldn't.

Reese sat down on the front step. He was sweating from his recent run. His head ached from lack of sleep and staying up late to finish writing his sperm bank story about the woman who'd taken Sabrina's place in the article.

A woman who had an agenda. She was the exact opposite of Sabrina. The woman was cold and calculating. Unlike Sabrina, the new subject hated men. Couldn't abide a man in her life.

But Sabrina had always wanted one. Ultimately her goal had been a family. She'd wanted a child before age made it more difficult for her to have one. She'd wanted to have someone to fill the lonely corners of her life.

Coward, he thought. He'd never acknowledged that loneliness played a part in his life. Now he realized how much he had been missing. How much would be missing again if he didn't do something to change the course his marriage was on. He had to do something more than make love to his beautiful wife.

She needed him to love her.

Could he? Was he the kind of man who could love? He'd have sworn he wasn't. He didn't know what it felt like. He only knew that when Sabrina said those three words to him, the world had stopped. His heartbeat had doubled and life hadn't seemed as lonely as it had before.

He had to go and find Sabrina. To talk to her. To see if there was some spark that he was misinterpreting that was love.

He stood up and entered the house. A radio played softly and the lights were warm and welcoming in the coming darkness. He walked through the house searching for her.

He found her curled on her side, sleeping on the couch. Sabrina's favorite Anita Baker CD was playing in the background. She wore one of his flannel shirts, her belly strained against the front of it. Her slim legs were encased in leggings and her reddish-brown hair was pulled up on top of her head.

Heat shot to his groin. And as he stood there he realized that it had also shot to his heart. That the organ he'd ignored forever and whose existence he'd denied had been there all the time. Alive and languishing. Needing only the right woman to show him how to use it, but at what cost?

He crossed to her and knelt at her side. She looked peaceful. He stared intently at her, trying to figure out what this love entailed.

She opened her eyes and screamed. Jerking upright, she covered her heart with her hand. She was so cute, he thought. Curls falling around her face, her breasts heaving as she struggled to catch her breath. She narrowed her eyes and glared at him.

"What?" he asked.

"What? You scared me half to death. What were you doing?"

"Watching you sleep."

"You couldn't do it from the chair across the room?"

"No, I couldn't." The answers he sought were the kind that needed up-close-and-personal observations.

"Reese, what's gotten into you?" she demanded.

"Nothing. But I'd like to get into you."

"Listen, whoever you are. I want my husband back."

"Don't be ridiculous, Sabrina."

"You're not a silly man, Reese. You're steady and serious and distant."

"Maybe I've changed."

"Doubtful." She pushed against his shoulder and

swung her legs to the floor. Reese stood and helped her to her feet.

"I'm serious, honey."

"Are you?"

"Yes."

"Well, then have a seat. I have something to tell you."

Her graveness struck him. What if she knew that he could never love her? Idiot! Of course she knows. That's why she stopped loving you. "You're not leaving again."

She sighed and shook her head. "No, I'm not. Not unless you ask me to."

"I'd never do that," he said.

"You can't foresee the future, Reese."

"No, I can't. Tell me your news."

"I'm sorry I didn't tell you sooner. I've just waited so long to talk about it, I'm nervous and I don't know how you'll react. But it happened a long—"

"Tell me," he said.

"You know I was married when I was eighteen." He nodded.

"Oh, God, Reese. I can't say it out loud."

"What is it?"

"I discovered I was pregnant."

"Did you give the child up?"

"No—never."

"What happened, baby?"

"Scott didn't want children. He wanted me to get an abortion and I refused."

"He ignored the pregnancy as if it never had occurred. When I was eight weeks along, he planned a camping trip for us. It was supposed to be our big reconciliation. I wanted my marriage to work but I was spotting.

"The doctor gave his okay and we went, but that night I miscarried the baby. Scott gloated, saying that he knew deep inside I didn't really want a child."

Sabrina buried her face in her hands.

Silence descended. Reese knew he should say something, but these were the kind of words he wasn't good at. She looked so lost and alone. The way he'd felt all his life.

"I'm sorry," he said. The words sounded inane.

"I've always wondered if maybe I could have done something more. This notion had haunted me. That maybe I put my marriage before my baby. And I was punished for it."

"Sabrina, I know you. No one in the world values—and deserves—a child more than you do."

"Thank you. I think I finally understand that the miscarriage wasn't my fault, but still I've been worrying about telling you."

"Why?"

"At first, because of the interviews. I mean, did I have a right to have a child after what had happened?"

"Sabrina, any woman as caring and nurturing as you are was meant to have a child."

"Oh, Reese. I love you," she said, laying her head on his chest.

He froze and realized whatever emotion he felt

for her ran deep. But he couldn't voice any words. Because he'd never wanted to be as vulnerable as Sabrina was at that moment. To know he held such power over her happiness floored him. He realized he couldn't give Sabrina the same power over him.

He'd never been able to give any woman that kind of power because he'd never really known a woman to treasure that kind of affection. His mother had loved him, but she'd given her life for his.

Knowing what pressure she'd put on herself to tell him about her past, she might not believe a declaration from him. The foolish happiness he'd been experiencing rushed right out of him. Would words be enough? He had a feeling it would take more to convince her he was a changed man.

"Reese, do you care for me at all?"

"Of course."

"But you don't love me." She said it plainly, as if she were only stating facts.

He couldn't hurt her any further, wouldn't even chance trying. He'd back out of her life slowly. Hell, it was the one thing he was really good at.

"No, honey, I can't love you."

She nodded and then quietly left the room. She took the light with her. The warmth and the CD shut off, and he stood alone in a room that had never felt like home until Sabrina had moved into it. He knew he'd made a big mistake but had no idea how to correct it.

Eleven

Sabrina had expected life to work out for the best, though experience had taught her there was no such thing as a "happy ending." But she'd been hedging her bets and hoping for one. The baby in her womb fulfilled her lifelong secret desire, and she wanted the rose-colored dream world she'd always envisioned.

Hearing Reese say that he couldn't love her turned those dreams to a nightmare. Two days later the words still lingered. The once-comfortable "American" dream of a perfect family in a house with a white picket fence had transformed into nothing more than a cold, beautiful home on the side of Mount Tam.

Her reality now consisted of the truth. The hard

facts that she'd done a good job of ignoring while she'd indulged her emotions in Reese. The truth she'd know before she saw that wonderful nursery. *The only things he was truly willing to give to her and the baby were material.*

The winter night was unnaturally dark, but a streetlight illuminated Reese's features. He drove the Lexus with casual ease. More ease than she'd have. It was with the same surety he did everything. Too bad that ease didn't extend to sealing the chilly wall she'd put between them.

It was hard to get over the fact that he'd said out loud what she'd known all along. She almost wished he'd never said he couldn't love her so she could've continued living in her fantasy.

"You really don't have to come in with me," she said into the quiet, acknowledging to herself that she was trying to needle him.

"I want to."

"Why? It's not as if—"

"Don't say it," he warned, his voice cutting through the layers of her own anger.

"I thought truth was important to you."

"It is."

"Well then, why can't I repeat what you said?"

"I don't want to hear it again."

She forced herself to look out the window. Sometimes it seemed as if he cared for her. The dark, shapeless shadows of the empty buildings took on a menacing feel as she let the loneliness she'd hoped to lose sweep over her.

Reese dropped her at the front of the women's

clinic for the evening Lamaze class and went to park the car. Christmas was only a few weeks away, and she thought of the previous year and the decisions she'd made. Decisions that had brought her to the insemination clinic and to Reese Howard. Suddenly, she realized she wouldn't change a thing. Reese had given her a dream come true and so much more. She'd learned about herself and had grown into the woman she'd always hoped to be by loving him.

The night breeze was biting. She huddled deeper into her coat, a recent gift from Reese, and watched for him. He strode briskly through the cold night looking at one with the darkness.

She was nervous. At first, having a child had seemed so right, and now as the time for the birth grew near, nerves and her uncomfortable body were making it impossible for her to sleep. She was scared that something would happen to the baby. That she'd do something and trigger a problem in the birth.

"Come on, honey," he said, cupping her elbow and leading her into the heated building.

She tugged her arm away from him.

"Please don't use endearments."

He grabbed her hand and pulled her into a small alcove. "What's with you tonight?"

"Nothing," she said.

She removed her coat as she walked down the hallway. The artificial warmth of the building surrounded her. Reese took her coat and draped it over his arm. He pulled her close, enveloping her in his heat. She wanted to submerge herself in the waves of warmth coming from him but she didn't. She had to think clearly about this man who couldn't love her. There was no real closeness between them except for the intimacy of lovers.

They sat together on one of the love seats provided in the room. Sabrina scanned the room, marveling at the different faces. Most of them looked like average-enough couples. A few of them were still in their teens and there was one expectant mother who had a friend with her instead of a significant other. Though her marriage wasn't the perfect dream she'd harbored, Reese was a stalwart of support.

She snuggled closer to him, regretting her petty anger of earlier. His arm tightened around her. He leaned down, brushing his lips against the top of her head. Why couldn't he love her?

Why did she have to sound like a virgin heroine in a gothic novel? Be brave and bold, she thought. Love him for all your worth and show him what he's missing.

But she'd tried that with her first marriage and it had backfired on her. She acknowledged to herself that an eighteen-year-old girl's all would be different than a thirty-year-old woman's.

And wasn't Reese worth the chance? she asked herself. Maybe she hadn't changed as much as she'd thought if she was still holding a part of herself back and not giving him her all. But she'd been trying to protect herself, and maybe that was why he couldn't love her.

The instructor came into the room and introduced

herself as Lori Mathers, a registered nurse with more than twenty years' experience in deliveries. As Lori talked about the process of natural childbirth, Sabrina sank deeper into the cushions and her husband. He stroked her arm and urged her to rest against him.

"I'm sorry," he whispered into her ear.

She glanced up at him, surprised and touched that he would apologize.

"I wish I could love you," he said, again softly.

She forced her attention back to the speaker. That was all she needed. She had to show Reese how to love her, and on the way home she planned to pursue this subject.

I wish I could love you.

The words echoed through his mind like the call of an orca whale to its mate Reese had once heard on a chilly morning, mist heavy in the air. The eerie sound played again and again. He never should have spoken out loud, but he had wanted to soothe the hurt he'd heard in her angry voice in the hallway.

The hurt he'd unintentionally inflicted on her time and again. He knew he'd deliberately tried to force her away from him a couple of times without thought to the pain she might feel. But he'd never expected to hurt over his actions, and he had. He felt a little like his dad and he hated that.

He knew that what he had with Sabrina was something rare and precious. If not for the emptiness deep inside him he'd be able to make it work.

How many times could he get away with pushing

her out of his life? He glanced over at his sleeping wife. Sabrina looked serene; like the ocean at dawn. But some latent childhood protective instinct warned that turbulence lay ahead. There was something about her tranquillity that touched him, soothing the fear and hurt left over from boyhood, and stretching into the present and the future. Sabrina was the key to overcoming his past, but he was afraid to trust her. Reese realized he was man enough to admit his fear to himself but would never be able to admit it to her.

Only recently had he realized how much he wanted to have the ability to care, which so many people took for granted. But those three little words evaded him. And he knew that when they were backed with true devotion just speaking them could change your life. Three words he'd never uttered.

He cursed his own lacking and forced his attention to the road. As the time for Sabrina to deliver the baby drew near, he worried about being away from her. The Lamaze class had been a bit on the gruesome side for him, showing a film called *Troubled Births*. He didn't need to see any other woman's birth experience to know what to do. He knew he didn't want to watch Sabrina in pain. His own mother must have been in terrible pain.

Though the film had ended with a saccharine-sweet father-mother-baby embrace, Reese was realistic enough to acknowledge that sometimes things went really wrong. He'd been reading books since Sabrina had confirmed she was going to have a baby—*his baby*. He thought he could deliver the baby himself if he had to.

He'd never had the security he found with Sabrina. It wasn't a feeling he could replicate on the volleyball court or on the sea. It came from her, and it made him feel warm inside. The thought of losing her and the small child growing inside her hurt him in a way he'd never realized he could hurt.

She dozed in the passenger seat of the Lexus while he drove home. The streetlights alternated between illuminating her pale face and hiding her in shadows. He felt as if they'd been doing a bit of the shadow tango in their marriage. Each reaching out for something they needed and then backing away before the other could realize the importance of that very thing. He knew it was time to step out of the shadows once and for all.

Sabrina had been tired lately. Probably because of him and his inability to love her. How many lives was Pete Howard going to ruin? His father had been reaching beyond the grave for years now.

Reaching out to beat Reese back whenever he tried to connect with a woman. Reaching out to stop Reese from making any meaningful human connection. He felt like the small boy who'd been locked time and again in a closet. Only this time he could see everything going on around him, but he still could not participate.

He saw how his attitude was affecting her. The pensive sadness he'd seen that one time in the kitchen as he'd left her home alone, had returned. It was there even when he was doing what she wanted him to do.

The pressure was almost too straining on his control. The control he'd used to protect himself and others from the destructive anger that had been core to his dad. That same dangerous feeling he'd felt roiling beneath his own surface only twice in his life, and one of those times was when Sabrina had tried to leave him. That scared him, because his control was the only thing keeping him from becoming the sick man that Pete Howard had been.

He should have never told her he couldn't love her. He knew it. But honesty was the one thing that he'd always had. It was the only thing he'd ever really had, and he didn't want to compromise even for her.

He pulled into the driveway and shut the car off. Laying his head on the steering wheel, he prayed for strength and guidance. Something he'd never done before.

He watched her sleeping for a few minutes, loathe to disturb her. The soft rasp of her breathing was soothing to his troubled thoughts. He was careful not to get in her face the way he had the other day. The nurse instructor had cautioned against exciting the expectant mothers.

He shook her gently. Even swollen with his child she was still a small woman. She always seemed fragile to him, which was ridiculous. She'd stood up to him in arguments, matched the strength of his passion in bed and loved him with quiet pride for the eight months of their marriage.

She shifted in her seat and blinked owlishly at him. "Are we home?"

"Yes," he said, opening the door and coming around to help her out of the car.

"My back aches," she said.

He imagined it did. Carrying around an extra twenty pounds had to be hard. "Let's go up to bed and I'll give you a back rub."

"I want to talk," she said.

"Good. I wasn't planning to be quiet."

"I'm serious, Reese."

"I know." And he did. That scared him. What could she possibly have to say to him? She'd been like quicksilver tonight, thoughtful one minute, angry the next, then at last gentle as a day-old kitten.

He didn't know how to handle her in this mood and that scared him. It scared him because he realized that he wanted her to stay with him for the next fifty years and keep loving him. Maybe he'd learn how to love her back and not lose himself.

Sabrina lay on her side on the wide king-size bed she shared with Reese. Though he'd been spending his nights down the hall in the guest bedroom lately, she had the feeling he'd be sleeping with her tonight. His massage wasn't as impersonal as she was sure he'd like it to be.

She watched his face reflected in the mirrored closet doors. He was intent on his task. His tanned hands looked big and masculine on her paler flesh. He was her opposite in so many ways.

Uncomfortable with her own nudity, she ignored

her form in the mirror. Reese had swept her night-shirt over her head and insisted she lie nude next to him. Insisted he help her smooth lotion onto her belly. And then insisted she talk to him while he rubbed scented oil into her skin.

She felt languid and lethargic. Not at all ready for a serious conversation, but there were questions she needed to ask, answers she needed to hear.

"I thought you wanted to talk," he said after a few minutes had passed.

"I do."

His hands smoothed down the line of her spine and lingered on her buttocks. She moved her hips more fully into his caress.

"Talk, Sabrina," he ordered.

She sought his eyes in the mirror and found him staring intently at her curving belly.

"Will you take your shirt off?" she asked. She loved his strength and the physical signs of it. His pecs were well-developed and his muscled stomach rippled when he did sit-ups every night. But his own strength was one of the things she knew he feared.

He removed the black flannel shirt and then settled himself closer behind her on the bed. His jeans-clad legs rested behind her hips. She sighed.

"Why can't you love me?" she asked.

He poured more oil into his palms and urged her onto her back. She realized she didn't want to look at her swollen body, though Reese did. In his eyes was a fire that couldn't be matched anywhere. He made her feel like the most sensual creature alive.

"I don't know how to love and cherish a

woman,'' he said, smoothing his hands over her breasts and belly.

She felt cherished, she realized as he said that he didn't know how. She realized that Reese was so used to being an anathema to everything good that he didn't recognize in himself the man he was.

Her breathing was shallow, and she knew she wouldn't be able to stay on her back for very long. She tried to sit up but it was a struggle. Reese helped her into a sitting position and handed her nightgown to her.

''Not that I wouldn't love to have you sitting there without a stitch on,'' he said.

She smiled at him; there was an edge to his words. She wondered if he resented her for being attractive to him. More than once she'd wanted to resent him for being the one man she hadn't been able to say no to.

''Do you care for me?'' she asked carefully. Not really sure how to get to the heart of the matter.

''I think I do. But I don't want to give you false hope. My entire life has been an emotional void and I'm comfortable in that void. To leave it now—''

He stared down at his callused hands. ''I just don't know how I'd survive.''

''I'll help you survive.''

He settled his hands on her shoulders and his expression was so grave that she nearly lost all hope. ''Sabrina, it's not a survival that you can help me with. It's inside, deep inside.''

''Everyone can love.''

''I can't.''

She thought about it for a moment. "What would be different if you loved me?"

"I don't know."

"Come on, Reese. I'm going to have to delve into the heart of you," she said, echoing the words he'd said that first afternoon they'd met.

"There is no heart, Sabrina. That's what I've been trying to tell you all along."

"Why did you push for marriage, then?"

"I wanted you to be mine. I wanted the baby to know the security of having a normal family."

"We're not a normal family."

"I was doing my duty, dammit. What a gentleman does," he said, vaulting off the bed and standing in front of her. His chest was heaving as if he'd run a marathon, and his eyes looked wild.

"You're not a gentleman, are you, Reese?"

"No, I'm not. But then you've known that all along."

"What's that mean?"

"You haven't really trusted me from the beginning. You always have one foot out the door, ready to leave if I don't live up to your expectations."

"It's hard not to have one foot out the door when you're always pushing me away."

He muttered an expletive.

"I've tried, Reese. Tried to show you what we could have if you'd only open yourself up to me, but you won't—no, you can't."

She swung her legs to the floor and struggled to her feet. Reese reached out to touch her and she glared at him.

He stood frozen, arm extended.

"I'm tired of the indecision. I want a family and more children and I want the man I love to be able to enjoy these things."

"I can't," he said.

"I know. I'm leaving, Reese. No wishy-washy thing like the last time. I'm not coming back unless something inside you changes. I'm not the scared girl I once was. Heck, I'm not even the same woman you married, the one who foolishly believed that if she was the perfect wife and mother she'd have the perfect marriage. I'm a woman who knows her worth, and if you can't love me then you are missing out on the chance of a lifetime."

With as much dignity as she could find, Sabrina walked to the bedroom door and held it open. "Please leave."

"Do you need a ride somewhere?" he asked quietly.

"No, I'll drive myself."

He nodded and walked into the darkened hallway. A man in shadows once more, she thought.

"I never meant to hurt you."

"Nor I you," she said softly. But he'd already walked away. No matter that she said she was the one leaving, somehow she was watching the one person she'd ever loved walk away.

She felt like she was dying inside but knew that she couldn't continue to love him and live with him while he tortured them both for not being a perfect ideal.

He lifted her in his arms and carried her to his car. This was all his fault. He should not have upset her. He was no better than his father. He shouldn't have let her try to leave. He couldn't lose her now.

He pulled his car phone from the glove box and settled Sabrina on the front seat. There was bloody fluid running down her legs and her eyes were wide and stricken.

"I can't lose another baby, Reese."

"I won't let you," he said, realizing he might not be able to save her or the baby. But he'd do everything within his power to protect them.

He dialed 911 as he drove toward the hospital. The dispatch operator was helpful and they had a police escort for the last three blocks before they arrived. Emergency room personnel rushed out of the automatic doors to take Sabrina into their care.

He followed blindly behind the gurney, needing desperately to retain some kind of contact with Sabrina. The doctor examined Sabrina while Reese held her hand. She was clinging to him. This woman who'd asked him for nothing but his love.

They shouldn't be here, he thought. He was in the emergency room! The damned emergency room instead of the state-of-the-art birthing center where they'd planned to have the baby. He knew that lots of women delivered before their due date, but Sabrina wasn't lots of women. She was his woman. The woman he couldn't live without.

He was tired of running from the truth. Sabrina was more important to him than he'd ever thought another person could be. He'd tried to deny it. Tried to ignore it, but all that effort had been wasted. Because even though he'd always believed he couldn't love, he knew that the ability had been there all along. Just waiting for the right woman to come along and unlock it.

He knew that with gut-wrenching surety, because what he'd been doing the last few weeks wasn't living. It was existing. And having tasted the slice of heaven that was Sabrina, he wanted her back, happy and healthy.

He held her hand, murmured gently to her until the doctor was finished with the examination. They'd hooked up a fetal monitor, and Reese didn't think he could breathe when the doctor reentered the room to talk to them.

Sabrina wouldn't let go of his hand. She was scared, he knew, and he also realized she needed him to be strong for her. "I'll be right here, honey."

"Mrs. Howard, your water broke when you fell. Please don't worry. We've got you hooked up to the fetal monitor, and I'm going to give you a drug that will induce your labor."

"Why?" Sabrina asked.

"The baby's heartbeat is faint and I don't want to take any chances."

She looked at him then, and Reese felt the bottom drop out of his world. He loved this woman more than life itself and he might lose her and their child.

Reese realized that the soul he'd thought he'd lost a long time ago was his again. As Sabrina watched him with pain-filled eyes, he knew that he'd trade his soul to take the pain from her. To make her comfortable and peaceful again.

They prepped her for birth, and as the process began, Reese felt a little uncomfortable and out of his element. But he'd gladly suffer those feelings in exchange for any comfort he could give Sabrina. He wanted to tell her he loved her. To wrap her in his embrace and declare himself to her, but a greater worry stopped him. Would Sabrina still love him after he'd driven her from their home and caused her to fall?

"Were you planning for an epidural?" the doctor asked.

"No, I'm going natural," Sabrina answered.

"Okay, here's what we're going to do. Dad, you watch the monitor and let Mom here know when a contraction is peaking. Mom, just relax and breathe. Your body knows what to do."

"Are you ready, honey?"

"I guess so," she said.

He bent and brushed a kiss against her forehead and then held her hand until the monitor beeped. "Okay, here comes a contraction."

Sabrina breathed like a trouper and Reese was glad when the contraction ended.

"I don't think I can do this," she said. The contractions kept growing stronger, the baby's heartbeat fainter and the doctor more agitated.

"I know, honey. I know."

"Reese, if something happens to me, you have to love our baby. Promise me right now that you'll say those words to our baby. Don't let him grow up without hearing those words.''

"Sabrina, I'm not going to let anything happen to you. I promise.''

"Some things can't be controlled. You taught me that," she said.

"Mom, let's get ready to push.''

The medical team worked around Sabrina, and Reese felt helpless as only a man can in this situation, he realized. He also knew there was no way he was going to let Sabrina give birth to his baby without telling her he loved her.

"Okay, Dad, watch the monitor and tell her when it's starting to peak.''

Sabrina was breathing and Reese was watching the monitor. "Now, honey.''

"Push, Mrs. Howard,'' the doctor commanded.

Sabrina struggled and grunted and Reese leaned closer, wrapping his arm around her shoulders to give her his strength.

"Looking good, Mom. Take a breather and we'll push one more time and have this little one delivered.''

Sabrina breathed heavily and Reese leaned down close to her, brushing his lips to her cheek. "I love you.''

Startled, she looked up at him, but the monitor beeped and it was time to push again. "Come on, Mom. One more time and…''

The doctor stopped talking as the baby slid from Sabrina's womb into his waiting hands. Reese's heart stopped for a moment as he looked from the crying baby to Sabrina.

He bent and kissed her startled lips. "We did it, honey."

She gave him one of her honest-to-goodness, from-the-heart smiles and held out her hands for the baby.

"Congratulations, Mom and Dad, you have a beautiful baby girl."

He was standing before her with tears in his eyes and a love so strong that it nearly filled the private room. And that love wasn't just directed at the child in her arms. She only hoped it wasn't too late. She acknowledged to herself that it wouldn't be too late. She needed Reese in her life the way she needed to breathe oxygen. Without it she would die.

"Oh, Reese," she said. More words were beyond her at that moment. His dark eyes blazed down at her and he, too, seemed unsure what to say.

She raised her free arm and touched the side of his face. The face that had always attracted her with its weathered and rough countenance. The face that was dearer to her than any other—except the small new one in her arms.

"Good work, little mother," he said, brushing a kiss on her forehead and wrapping his one hand under the baby. He had the other arm around her shoulder, and she realized he was protecting his small family. Reese was a man who was capable of always protecting the three of them, and not just from external threats.

He'd always protected her from what he saw as the greatest danger—himself.

Sabrina cuddled her new daughter close to her chest. She found herself unable to look away from her husband's dark eyes. She was tired, but his hand in hers felt so right. Just as his eyes had seemed on that first sunny afternoon when they'd met.

Yin to her yang.

Reese Howard shared more than an ordinary love with her. He shared a bonding of souls and a small miracle. Sabrina shivered at the feeling of satisfaction that thought brought.

"She's cold over here, can we get some more blankets?" Reese asked one of the orderlies.

Sabrina smiled to herself. He was still taking charge and ordering things for her that he thought she needed. He was scrutinizing the poor young man who scurried to get another blanket for her.

"Reese?"

"Yes, honey."

"I love you."

"I know," he said, and the quiet satisfaction in his voice made her smile.

"You don't have to sound so arrogant."

"I know," he repeated.

"You love me?" she asked, unsure what else to say.

"More than I'd ever thought possible."

"Oh, Reese."

He smiled rather indulgently at her. But there was a sadness that bothered her.

"You're not blaming yourself for my fall, are

you?'' she demanded, knowing him well enough to see the guilt beneath the sadness.

''If I hadn't—''

''No. I won't let you do it. You're a good, kind man, Reese Howard, and I won't have anyone, even you, thinking otherwise.''

Her eyelids felt heavy and she couldn't keep them open. ''Don't go away, Reese.''

''I won't,'' he said. And the quiet assurance in his words should have enabled her to rest.

She closed her eyes promising herself only a minute. Too much was left unsaid between them, and she needed to settle matters. To find out if the love she saw in his eyes was real.

Annabelle cried softly, and Sabrina opened her eyes and scanned the room. Reese stood, looking out the window with the baby nestled in his strong arms. He was murmuring softly to their child.

Nothing had ever touched her like the sight of her husband and child. She'd remember the tears in his eyes for the rest of her life.

''Reese?''

''Annabelle and I have been waiting for you to wake up.''

''Is she hungry?'' Sabrina asked as Reese walked toward her.

''I think so, but maybe she was only lonely.''

Only lonely. His words touched her. They described so clearly the two of them. She took her daughter from him when he handed her over. She unbuttoned the front of her gown and settled the baby at her breast.

Reese watched her with a combination of tenderness and lust.

"Ready to talk?" she asked, afraid he'd leave before they could.

"Sure."

"Do you still love me?" she asked, needing reassurance.

"Yes."

"Since when?"

"Oh, this is going to be one of those discussions," he said teasingly. It was a glimpse of the man she'd seen on a few occasions and she wanted to see more of him.

She just looked at him, waiting for her answer.

"I think since the first moment I met you. I kept trying to put you into a familiar niche, but you wouldn't fit."

"Me, too. You scared me because what I felt for you is more intense than anything I've ever felt before."

"I know. Finally, I know what you mean. These last three weeks have been torture, and though I know that I should let you go so you can find a decent guy, I can't."

"Good, because I think you are a decent guy."

"Really?"

"Of course."

"I love you, honey."

His words were sincere and honest, melting the last of her doubts. Standing beside her was the man she'd always knew he could be. The Reese she'd seen glimpses of in the past—her battle-weary warrior finally returned to home.

''I know,'' she said, echoing his words earlier, and though she was new to that kind of arrogance she thought she did quite well.

He laughed quietly. Sabrina switched Annabelle to her other breast.

''You know, for a reporting assignment that started out annoying me, this has been the best thing to ever happen to me.''

''I know.''

He smiled down at her, no longer a man in shadows, but a man who was finally in sunlight. *Her man.* And as he brought his hand up to caress their sleeping daughter's head, she knew with absolute certainty that Reese was her soul mate.

''I want more kids,'' Sabrina said.

I know, he thought...*and so do I,* he realized happily.

Epilogue

The *Time Lapse,* which had once served as his escape from a lonely world, was now filled with laughter and song. His children played on the deck, and his wife piloted the boat with an ease she'd learned only after years of practice.

"Daddy, look at me," Annabelle called to him from her perch on the ropes. Wind blew through her reddish-brown hair, and he knew this was what Sabrina had looked like as a young girl.

Their firstborn had just turned seven. Four-year-old Caleb wasn't far behind her. Reese grabbed both of his kids and held them over the Pacific Ocean.

"Who wants a swim?" he asked.

Childish giggles filled the air, and Reese felt a

sense of contentment he wouldn't have believed the world offered before he'd met Sabrina. She'd turned into his light and his life. Soothing him in ways the dangerous stunts he'd pulled in the past never had.

They were sailing down to Santa Barbara for the Cal King Tournament, which he and Jeff had a good chance at winning this year. Life was full and rich and good, Reese decided.

He set the kids on the deck with a warning to stay off the ropes and went to stand behind his beloved wife.

Her body was reed-slim despite two births and a third pregnancy. Though she was only two months along, her breasts were exquisitely sensitive.

"How are you feeling?" he asked as he slipped up behind her, resting his hands on her hips.

"Good. I love being at sea."

Her hair fanned out from her scalp, teasing his face. He leaned closer, inhaling the scent of his woman, holding her with a fierceness he'd never be able to control.

"I love you," he said softly. The words came easier to him now.

"I love you, too," she said.

The love in her eyes shone for the world to see, and he proudly accepted that Sabrina was his mate in every way. Holding his wife in his arms while his children played a few feet away, Reese felt the happiness he'd been searching for all his life surround and engulf him. No matter what the seas of

life offered them, he and his family would steer their
course together.

*   *   *   *   *

*As Katherine Garbera's emotional story
just proved, funny things really can happen
on the way to the sperm bank!*

*Don't miss talented author
Metsy Hingle's sensuous love story,*

THE BABY BONUS,

*available May 2000—another delightful
tale in Silhouette Desire's promotion*

THE BABY BANK:

*Where love is measured
in pounds and ounces!*

Look Who's Celebrating Our 20th Anniversary:

Celebrate 20 YEARS

"Silhouette Desire is the purest form of contemporary romance."
—*New York Times* bestselling author
Elizabeth Lowell

"Let's raise a glass to Silhouette and all the great books and talented authors they've introduced over the past twenty years. May the *next* twenty be just as exciting and just as innovative!"
—*New York Times* bestselling author
Linda Lael Miller

"You've given us a sounding board, a place where, as readers, we can be entertained, and as writers, an opportunity to share our stories.... You deserve a special round of applause on...your twentieth birthday. Here's wishing you many, many more."
—International bestselling author
Annette Broadrick

Silhouette Desire

SILHOUETTE'S 20TH ANNIVERSARY CONTEST
OFFICIAL RULES
NO PURCHASE NECESSARY TO ENTER

1. To enter, follow directions published in the offer to which you are responding. Contest begins 1/1/00 and ends on 8/24/00 (the "Promotion Period"). Method of entry may vary. Mailed entries must be postmarked by 8/24/00, and received by 8/31/00.

2. During the Promotion Period, the Contest may be presented via the Internet. Entry via the Internet may be restricted to residents of certain geographic areas that are disclosed on the Web site. To enter via the Internet, if you are a resident of a geographic area in which Internet entry is permissible, follow the directions displayed on-line, including typing your essay of 100 words or fewer telling us "Where In The World Your Love Will Come Alive." On-line entries must be received by 11:59 p.m. Eastern Standard time on 8/24/00. Limit one e-mail entry per person, household and e-mail address per day, per presentation. If you are a resident of a geographic area in which entry via the Internet is permissible, you may, in lieu of submitting an entry on-line, enter by mail, by hand-printing your name, address, telephone number and contest number/name on an 8"x 11" plain piece of paper and telling us in 100 words or fewer "Where In The World Your Love Will Come Alive," and mailing via first-class mail to: Silhouette 20ᵗʰ Anniversary Contest, (in the U.S.) P.O. Box 9069, Buffalo, NY 14269-9069; (In Canada) P.O. Box 637, Fort Erie, Ontario, Canada L2A 5X3. Limit one 8"x 11" mailed entry per person, household and e-mail address per day. On-line and/or 8"x 11" mailed entries received from persons residing in geographic areas in which Internet entry is not permissible will be disqualified. No liability is assumed for lost, late, incomplete, inaccurate, nondelivered or misdirected mail, or misdirected e-mail, for technical, hardware or software failures of any kind, lost or unavailable network connection, or failed, incomplete, garbled or delayed computer transmission or any human error which may occur in the receipt or processing of the entries in the contest.

3. Essays will be judged by a panel of members of the Silhouette editorial and marketing staff based on the following criteria:

   > Sincerity (believability, credibility)—50%
   >
   > Originality (freshness, creativity)—30%
   >
   > Aptness (appropriateness to contest ideas)—20%

   Purchase or acceptance of a product offer does not improve your chances of winning. In the event of a tie, duplicate prizes will be awarded.

4. All entries become the property of Harlequin Enterprises Ltd., and will not be returned. Winner will be determined no later than 10/31/00 and will be notified by mail. Grand Prize winner will be required to sign and return Affidavit of Eligibility within 15 days of receipt of notification. Noncompliance within the time period may result in disqualification and an alternative winner may be selected. All municipal, provincial, federal, state and local laws and regulations apply. Contest open only to residents of the U.S. and Canada who are 18 years of age or older, and is void wherever prohibited by law. Internet entry is restricted solely to residents of those geographical areas in which Internet entry is permissible. Employees of Torstar Corp., their affiliates, agents and members of their immediate families are not eligible. Taxes on the prizes are the sole responsibility of winners. Entry and acceptance of any prize offered constitutes permission to use winner's name, photograph or other likeness for the purposes of advertising, trade and promotion on behalf of Torstar Corp. without further compensation to the winner, unless prohibited by law. Torstar Corp and D.L. Blair, Inc., their parents, affiliates and subsidiaries, are not responsible for errors in printing or electronic presentation of contest or entries. In the event of printing or other errors which may result in unintended prize values or duplication of prizes, all affected contest materials or entries shall be null and void. If for any reason the Internet portion of the contest is not capable of running as planned, including infection by computer virus, bugs, tampering, unauthorized intervention, fraud, technical failures, or any other causes beyond the control of Torstar Corp. which corrupt or affect the administration, secrecy, fairness, integrity or proper conduct of the contest, Torstar Corp. reserves the right, at its sole discretion, to disqualify any individual who tampers with the entry process and to cancel, terminate, modify or suspend the contest or the Internet portion thereof. In the event of a dispute regarding an on-line entry, the entry will be deemed submitted by the authorized holder of the e-mail account submitted at the time of entry. Authorized account holder is defined as the natural person who is assigned to an e-mail address by an Internet access provider, on-line service provider or other organization that is responsible for arranging e-mail address for the domain associated with the submitted e-mail address.

5. Prizes: Grand Prize—a $10,000 vacation to anywhere in the world. Travelers (at least one must be 18 years of age or older) or parent or guardian if one traveler is a minor, must sign and return a Release of Liability prior to departure. Travel must be completed by December 31, 2001, and is subject to space and accommodations availability. Two hundred (200) Second Prizes—a two-book limited edition autographed collector set from one of the Silhouette Anniversary authors: Nora Roberts, Diana Palmer, Linda Howard or Annette Broadrick (value $10.00 each set). All prizes are valued in U.S. dollars.

6. For a list of winners (available after 10/31/00), send a self-addressed, stamped envelope to: Harlequin Silhouette 20ᵗʰ Anniversary Winners, P.O. Box 4200, Blair, NE 68009-4200.

Contest sponsored by Torstar Corp., P.O. Box 9042, Buffalo, NY 14269-9042.

PS20RULES

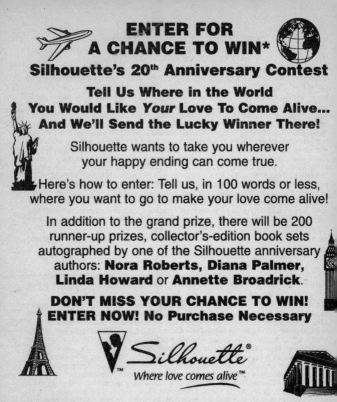